J. M. Hood

New Lights

Spirits unbottled

J. M. Hood

New Lights
Spirits unbottled

ISBN/EAN: 9783337272449

Printed in Europe, USA, Canada, Australia, Japan

Cover: Foto ©Andreas Hilbeck / pixelio.de

More available books at **www.hansebooks.com**

OR,

SPIRITS UNBOTTLED.

A COMEDY IN FIVE ACTS.

D.

Cop 1878.

All pe
f

NEW LIGHTS;

OR,

SPIRITS UNBOTTLED.

A COMEDY IN FIVE ACTS.

"Thus runs the world away."—SHAKSPEARE.

ACT I.—"At the Oaks."—New Lights begin to glimmer.

ACT II.—The Servant of the Spheres pays a little of his attention to the Investigator. "Come, let us reason together."

ACT III.—In the garden.—A new light shines with a lurid glare.

ACT IV.—"At Magnolia."—Mrs. Sniffen entertains angels unawares.

ACT V.—Dr. Mann as a special constable. "I am here for a purpose."

An interval of two years between Acts III. and IV.

ABBREVIATIONS USED.— R., (right); R. D., (right door); R. C., (right of centre); C., (centre); R. U. C., (right upper centre); L., (left); L. D., (left door); L. C., (left of centre); L. U. C., (left upper centre); D. C., (down centre); U. C., (up centre); A., (arch); L. 1 E., (left first entrance); L. 2 E., (left second entrance); 1 v., (first vase); 2 v., (second vase); W., (window); C. A., (centre arch); R. A., (right arch); L. A., (left arch).

DRAMATIS PERSONÆ.

PROFESSOR CONFUCIUS CROWELL, a Servant of the Spheres.
JUDGE ERLY, an Investigator.
REGINALD ERLY, Heir to "The Oaks."
VOLTAIRE DARWIN, a Genuine Medium.
ST. ELMO SNIFFEN, the "Royally Endowed."
THOMAS, Servant at "The Oaks."
ROMEO, Colored Servant at "Magnolia."

FREDERICA MANN, M.D., A Self-made Man.
MRS. ERLY, a Veritable Martyr.
DAISY LORIMER, a Little Nobody.
NINA DARE, Judge Erly's Ward.
MRS. SNIFFEN, a Woman of Sentiment.
ELLEN, a Lady Help.
ANGELICA CELESTIA SNIFFEN, the "Bud of Promise."
Walking ladies and gentlemen.

COSTUMES AND PROPERTIES.

CROWELL.—Worn and ill-fitting black clothes. Crushed beaver hat. Turned down shirt collar and loose tie. Hair brushed back from a bald forehead and worn very long. Octagonal rimmed spectacles. A couple of valises with books, photographs, a bottle, "planchette," etc. Picture of a "Spirit-Bride," and a map of a "Plan of the Universe" mounted on rollers. Silver spoons in valise for Act III. Linen coat Act III. *Second Costume (Act V.).* Same as before, with flowered velvet waistcoat, bright-colored neck-handkerchief, large button-hole bouquet, yellow gloves and gaudy handkerchief added.

REGINALD ERLY.—Riding costume, with top-boots, whip or cane, hat, gloves, etc. *Second Costume (Act II.).* Home costume. Revolver ready for Act III. *Third Costume (Act IV.).* Travelling costume. Hat, gloves, etc. *Fourth Costume (Act V.).* Evening dress.

JUDGE ERLY.—Flowered dressing-gown ; slippers ; skull-cap. *Second Costume (Act III.).* Long fur coat ; fur cap. *Third Costume (Act IV.).* Travelling costume. *Fourth Costume (Act V.).* Evening dress.

VOLTAIRE DARWIN.—Tall, pale, and somewhat wild-looking. Hair worn long. Black clothes. Turned-down collar and loose tie. Gloves, cane, slouched sombrero.

ST. ELMO.—Evening dress. Hair in long curls.

THOMAS.—Servant's livery.

ROMEO.—Dress of a colored servant at the South.

FREDERICA MANN.—Wears a blonde wig of short curling hair. Coat, vest, trousers and short skirt of gray cloth, embroidered with blue. Ruffled shirt. Blue tie. Handkerchief, gloves, cane, etc. Ladies' riding hat or boy's straw hat. Cigar-case, note-books, circulars, cards, etc. *Second Costume (Act IV.).* Suitable for "half-mourning." *Third Costume (Act V.).* Trousers, skirt, and cut-away coat of blue satin. Vest of white satin embroidered with silver. Lace ruffles, diamond pin, handkerchief, button-hole bouquet, gloves, etc. Blue silk hose, shoes with straps and buckles. A pair of handcuffs ready for Act V.

DAISY LORIMER.—White silk grenadine dress. Scarlet flowers in hair. Mantilla or scarf of white lace fastened to hair with flowers, or jeweled pin may be worn in the garden scene Act III. A letter ready in Act II. *Second Costume (Act IV.).* Simple but elegant mourning.

NINA DARE.—Rich home costume. Changes of dress in Acts II. and III. if desired. *Second Costume (Act IV.).* Travelling dress. *Third Costume (Act V.).* Full evening dress and rich jewelry.

MRS. SNIFFEN.—House costume. Eye-glasses. Fan. Handkerchief. *Second Costume (Act V.)* Full evening dress.

MRS. ERLY.—Home costume. Carries a watch. Knitting-work.

ELLEN.—Wig of red or auburn hair. Cambric dress with apron and cap coquettishly worn. Dusters, etc. *Second Costume (Act IV.).* Travelling dress. *Third Costume (Act V.).* Full evening dress and rich jewelry.

ANGELICA CELESTIA.—White dress. Colored Sash. Hair in long braids. *Second Costume (Act V.).* Evening dress of lace and muslin worn over silk. Silk hose, kid slippers, handkerchief, fan, gloves, etc.

[Walking ladies and gentlemen in evening dress.]

ACT I.

Scene.—*A drawing room at " The Oaks." Conservatory at rear, visible through arch. Practicable fire-place* (R.). *Cabinet with bric-a-brac* (L.). *Table with chairs placed beside it* (L. C.). *Sofa* (R. U. C.). *Easy chair in front of fire-place. Bell-rope* (L.) *Chairs, pictures, vases, etc. Small table in corner* (L.).

Properties.—*Thermometer on wall* (L.). *China pitcher and Japanese fans on mantel* (R.). *Books on table, writing materials etc.* (L. C.). *Punch bowl, bottles; a salver with food and rich coffee service ready for* Thomas *at right entrance. Warming-pans, bottles, etc., ready for* Ellen *at right entrance.*

As curtain rises, Ellen *is discovered dusting ornaments on mantel.*

Ellen (R.)—There now! everything's as bright as hands can make it, and yet I'll be bound the old tomcat'll find something or other to have particular fits about. I just wish I had the training of him for a while, the irritating, aggravating, cantankerous old bull-frog!

[*Enter* Thomas L. C.]

Thomas (L. D.).—Going it again like a tempest in a coal-scuttle, be you, Miss Prandergast? I say it's lucky there ain't no ducking-stools for scolds nowadays.

El. (R. C.).—Hain't I got reason to scold, with an old hypo. for a master, and nobody but a fool like you to keep company with?

Thos.—I may be a fool, but I tell you what—the master is a man what knows how to keep the whip-hand of a woman.

El.—The old vampire, a-worrying the poor mistress into an unseemly grave! If he was under my thumb, Thomas, he wouldn't feel so chipper! I'd like to see the man—Turk or Chinee—that would *dare* to trample on me!

Thos.—I always did admire you for your spunk, Ellen, and if you'll only name the happy day 'twill suit you to become Mrs. Thomas Green, you'll make sure of having your own way in everything for the rest of your days.

El.—I'd have to be a sight *greener* than I am now. I let you know, Mr. Thomas, that I look much higher. [*Struts about making her short gown trail.*] I feel it in me to trail my silks and satins, and, like as not, to splash *you* with my carriage mud.

Thos.—Ain't I as good as you be, Ellen? We're fellow-servants.

El.—You needn't *Ellen* me, Mr. Green, for my name takes a *Miss* before it as well as another; and as for my being a servant, I call myself a lady help.

Thos.—You've encouragited me, many's the occasion I could name. Come now, kiss and make up. [*Approaches nearer.*]

El. — As if I'd let the likes of you kiss me, Mr. Impudence!

[Thomas *appears to struggle for a kiss, and* Ellen *to resist him.*]

Thos.—[*Jumping about*] Ouw! ouw! You gave me an awful dig, you spit-fire! You red-head! Ouw! ouw!

El.—Ha! ha! ha! Roses has thorns, Mr. Thomas! But, hush! here comes master.

[*Enter* Judge Erly (l. d.).]

Judge Erly (l. u. c.).—What is the meaning of this disturbance? I shall discharge you from my service for your disgraceful conduct, young woman.

El.—[*Sobbing*] Indeed, it wasn't my fault. He—he—tried to—to kiss me!

THOS.—And she digged me awful, sir; she's got a nasty temper.

JUDGE.—[*Crossing R. and seating himself near fire-place*]. I wish she had scratched your eyes out. Go directly for my lunch, you unconscionable idiot!

[*Exit* THOMAS (L. D.).]

Ellen, you may inform Mrs. Erly——

EL. (L. U. C.).—That you're wanting a little of her attention? Yes, sir; I'll tell her, sir. [*Exit* L. D.].

JUDGE.—The saucy baggage! How in thunder did *she* know what I was about to say? [*As if in pain*] Oh! o-h! my poor fluttering heart! No one knows what I have to endure, for I never complain.

[*Enter* MRS. ERLY, L. D.]

MRS. ERLY (C.).—Have they made you quite comfortable, my dear?

JUDGE.—Comfortable? The house as cold as a barn, and the servants off, no one knows where. Because I never complain, you all think that I need no attention.

[MRS. ERLY *seats herself* L. C. *and takes out knitting.*]

MRS. E.—Is there anything I can do for you, my dear?

JUDGE.—Nothing, except to give me a few minutes of your attention. Where is Rex? I've come down for the sole purpose of having a serious talk with the boy.

MRS. E.—Rex went riding with Miss Lorimer more than two hours ago; I dare say they will soon be here.

JUDGE.—With Miss Lorimer! Blood and thunder, ma'am; this thing must be put a stop to! Suppose Rex should take it into his head to fall in love with Miss Lorimer?

MRS. E.—Of course, there would be serious objections to——

JUDGE.—Serious objections! Fiends and furies, ma'am, if he should take a notion to marry the girl, it would be stark, staring ruin!

MRS. E.—After all, my dear, we have no control over Rex, and——

JUDGE.—No control! We can pack Miss Daisy Lorimer off, ma'am, bag and baggage, before the boy makes an idiot of himself! But here comes the young rascal now.

[*Enter* REGINALD ERLY *through* A.]

REGINALD (D. C.).—I am pleased to see you in the drawing-room, my dear uncle.

JUDGE.—The deuce you are! Sit down, sir; I've something serious to say to you.

REG.—[*Aside*] Then it's sure to be disagreeable. [*Seats himself near* JUDGE.]

JUDGE.—Ahem! You aunt tells me, Rex, that you have been out riding with Miss Lorimer again?

REG.—[*Aside*] I'm in for it! [*Aloud*] I have had that pleasure, sir.

JUDGE.—Now, Rex, it won't do—it won't do!

REG.—What will not do, sir?

JUDGE.—This paying attention to Miss Lorimer. It will put notions in her head. You'll have her falling in love with you.

REG.—I'm sure I've no objections.

JUDGE.—What, you young villain! Daisy is too nice a little girl to be made 'a fool of.

REG.—I agree with you, sir.

JUDGE.—You can't marry her—you know that. She's a mere nobody without family or fortune—no prospects but to bundle to the almshouse when her mummy of a grand-marm dies.

REG.—I have made up my mind to marry her if she will accept me.

JUDGE.—Are you mad? Do you suppose that Nina Dare is going to refuse you? Or have you forgotten that, according to the imbecile condition of your father's drivelling will, you are bound to propose to her within six months?

REG.—Or forfeit a fortune to be shared with her. I prefer the alternative. Possibly my father had a right to enrich whom he pleased, but he certainly had no right to dispose of my hand.

JUDGE.—If you persist in this folly, you'll be a poor penniless devil all your days.

REG.—Not so bad as that. I shall still be owner of "The Oaks." Then there are the family diamonds—and the plate. And you forget my profession, uncle. Am I not a rising young lawyer?

[*Enter* NINA DARE *through* A.]

JUDGE.—Come, sir, no more of this idle talk. You must forget your puppy love and marry your father's heiress.

REG.—Never! I have no regard for Nina. I am suspicious of her past life. I dislike the sort of people of whom she makes her friends and confidants. Would you have me marry such a woman rather than make the pecuniary sacrifice my honor demands?

JUDGE.—Then strychnine her coffee if you've got the nerve to do it, and I swear I'll tell no tales! [*Coughs.*]

NINA (D. C.).—Am I the subject of dispute as usual? [*Seats herself near* MRS. ERLY.]

MRS. E.—Dear! dear! how much trouble there is in this world!

[*Enter* ELLEN, R. D., *holding door closed as if trying to keep some one back.*]

EL.—Such queer folks, and they would follow me to the drawing room!

[*Knocking at the door.*]

Some sort of a self-made man, I reckon, and an agent.

JUDGE.—Turn 'em out, you imbecile! Aren't my orders that agents shall not be admitted to the house at all?

EL.—But they say they will see Miss Dare.

[*The door is opened and* ELLEN *pushed rudely aside.*]

[*Enter* PROFESSOR CROWELL *first, and* DR. MANN *second,* R. D.]

NI.—[*Rising*] I have business with these people, and will receive them elsewhere.

REG.—[*Aside*] Business! [*Takes a book from table and seats himself* L. 'U. C.]

JUDGE.—Who the Devil are you, intruding yourselves into a gentleman's drawing-room in this shameless manner?

PROF. CROWELL.—[*Bowing profoundly*] My good friend, why adjure us in the name of an Antiquated Myth of a Fossilized Theology? Let us reason together. [*Puts his valises under sofa.*]

DR. MANN.—To be sure! the devil, indeed! Why, man alive, the fish-god of India is quite as respectable.

JUDGE.—I want to know your business here.

DR. M.—[*Handing circular*] Permit me to introduce myself: Frederica Mann, Electro-magnetic and Common-sense Physician, as you will see by my circular. The gentleman who accompanies me is Professor Confucius Crowell, also a Healer of the flesh.

[*Seats herself* R. *tipping chair back to the wall and placing hat on the floor beside her.*]

PROF. C.—You see in me, my good friend, an humble servant of the spheres. (D. C.) I lift up my voice as a Vindicator of the Truth, and an Emancipator of the Creed-bound. I come to bid you one and all be free! Shake off the manacles of those Giant Opposers to Progress, Superstition and Prejudice! Why longer cling to Rotten Systems, tamely submitting to be mineral-drugged and priest-ridden? Am I obscure, or are ye, O my hearers, obtuse?

JUDGE.—I insist upon knowing your business here. You may be people of the worst possible repute—indeed, I think it highly probable that you are.

DR. M.—Old gentleman, our business is with Miss Dare.

PROF. C.—[*Bowing profoundly*] I believe we are addressing ourselves to her guardian, Judge Erly, surrounded by his amiable family?

JUDGE.—Humph! deuced amiable! You say that you have business with Miss Dare, young woman. Wherever did my ward make your acquaintance?

DR. M.—Maplewood Academy, some five years ago. I was then Fred. Lawless, a young orphan pupil, paying my way by teaching the terpsichorean art and calisthenics.

JUDGE.—Humph! Were you permitted to wear your present nondescript attire while at Maplewood?

[*During the following conversation* PROFESSOR *takes a small stand from the left corner, seats himself with it* (L.C.) *and makes it tip as if in answer to imaginary questions. Becomes excited and pushes it about the room in a lively manner, followed by* ELLEN, *who finally captures and replaces it.*]

DR. M.—By no means. Mrs. Grundy was omnipotent at the Academy. Now I go in for comfort and don't care a square-toed pope for the opinions of all creation.

JUDGE.—You were a single woman at that time, I take it?

DR. M.—Just so, and have been married and widowed since —my luck! You see, when I left Maplewood I invested all I had in a kindergarten. It was a great success. Children made rapid progress, parents delighted, press enthusiastic, and so on! But, unfortunately it was a failure *financially.* I burned a few more holes in my pockets trying experiments, then took a ticket in the matrimonial lottery.

JUDGE.—[*Aside*] Humph! an adventuress.

[*Enter* THOMAS *carrying salver* (R. D.).]

DR. M.—I drew a prize. The late doctor and your humble were as happy as turtle-doves and all that sort of thing, but the man had to up and die. Financially, my marriage was a failure; my good husband left me nothing but his practice.

THOS.—Your lunch is served, sir. [*Places salver on table.*]

[PROFESSOR *and* JUDGE *approach table.*]

DR. M.—I've no grounds for complaint, however. Financially, my profession is a success. I've an army of patients in Boston.

JUDGE.--Humph! an army in the grave-yards, more likely.

DR. M.—Ha! ha! ha! I see you must have your little jokes.

JUDGE.—The meat is a mess—a villanous mess! If I had my strength, I'd horse-whip the cook within a hair's breadth of his life. How often have I told the black rascal that meat tastes like a mouse—*precisely* like a mouse, stewed in this diabolical fashion.

[*Exit* THOMAS (R. D.).]

PROF. C.--[*Eating the meat.*] It is indeed very like mouse.

JUDGE.--What the devil do you know of the flavor of a mouse, sir? [*Crosses to his seat* (R.).]

PROF. C.--Everything. I once ran an eating house for the benefit of the starving poor of a great city. I served delicious and nutricious stews of cat, rat, mouse, dog and horse flesh, for a mere song. But, my good friend, prejudice is a curious thing.

DR. M.—[*Crossing to table*] A mob threatened Confucius, and the police closed up the philanthropical concern. Pity! for it promised to be a great success financially.

PROF. C.--But the world moves, my good Dr. Mann, the world moves.

DR. M.--I'll wager my last dollar that you're a dyspeptic, Judge Erly.

JUDGE.—Humph! You've no understanding of my case whatever, ma'am. I am the victim of an affection of the heart; I believe it to be ossification, a disease but little understood by the ordinary physician. Ah! nobody knows what I suffer, for I am one of that sort of people who never complain.

DR. M.—[*Poking at food with her walking stick*] My pet hobby is dietetic reform. Why, bless you, man, your heart is all right—it's your liver. Now here's pastry! Faugh!

PROF. C.—[*Eating the pastry*] Pastry is by no means injurious to all constitutions.

DR. M.—Why eat meat at all?—you're not a ghoul. As for coffee, it's slow poison.

PROF. C.—[*Drinking the coffee*] Very slow. I shall continue to be a lingering suicide.

DR. M.—[*Crossing to seat* (R.)] Graham cakes, prunes, oat-meal is the food that you want. I'd have you as sound as a button in no time if you'd obey my orders.

JUDGE. —Ma'am, I'd as soon think of consulting with a cat as a female physician. Do you belong to the regular medical faculty, Professor Crowell?

DR. M.—Oh, Confucius is regular enough! Bought a diploma of a Philadelphia broker once on a time. Excuse me, Crowell; one of the little jokes I must have.

PROF. C.—Sir, I am no ordinary physician bound by the legends of a murderous practice. On the contrary, I am bitterly opposed to the Calomel Poisoners and Blood-letting Vampires of the Old School, college-bred and diplomatized though they may be. Of what avail is the learned ignorance of the foolish? The Regulars, jealous of our successes, are seeking through tyrannous laws to bind the hands of the Inspired Healer with manacles of iron.

JUDGE.—Am I to understand that you are what is called a Medium—a Clairvoyant?

PROF. C.—I am, sir. The most carefully guarded secrets of nature are revealed to me when my mind is held in apogee by my Medicine Band. I, and such as I, are the Precursors of the Doom of Bigotry, the Forerunners of the lifting of the Veil of Mystery, the Harbingers of New Lights. What has Orthodoxy done for this world, sir? Let us reason together. Orthodoxy has kept the Spirits of the Departed bottled up for centuries, and hermetically sealed. I come to tell you they are free—as free as light, as free as air, sir. They float about us sympathizing with our griefs, and sharing our joy.

JUDGE.—That's a beautiful belief.

PROF. C.—It isn't belief, it's knowledge. We don't believe anything, we *know*. It's your orthodox folks who demand heads full of credulity. Are you conscious of the fact, sir, that the spirit of a Beautiful Woman is hovering above your head at this very moment?

JUDGE.—[*Starting*] What the devil! you don't tell me so.

PROF. C.—And I count six other disembodied spirits in this room at this very moment. Ah! truly, my good friend, we must soar on the wings of the inspirational, if we would pierce the impenetrable.

REG. (D. C.).—You insult our understandings, sir.

PROF. C.—[*Facing Reginald*] A—ha! young man, I read you! You would make of yourself a stumbling-block to trip up the Would-be Investigators of Truth—those Infant Giants in the Divine Arcana of Thought.

DR. M.—Come, come, good folks, let's all keep our tempers! No use in getting excited. [*Taking out cigar-case.*] Is there any objection to my smoking?

REG.—Most assuredly, madam. There is a lady in the room—my aunt, Mrs. Erly.

NI.—[*Aside*] Insolence!

DR. M.—Ha! ha! ha! You object to the coming woman, Erly?

REG.—I pray that she may be kept back as long as possible.

PROF. C.—O hoary prejudice!

JUDGE.—I was about to remark, Professor Crowell, that, deeply as I am interested in the phenomena of spiritualism, I have never before met with a medium of any sort.

PROF. C.—Is it possible? But the truth is spreading. We Mediums, more correctly called Sensitives, will soon permeate this globe from pole to pole—"From Greenland's icy mountains," to "India's coral strand," to quote the poet.

JUDGE.—Are you what is called a materializing medium?

PROF. C.—I am, sir. In my Magnetic Aura, Spirits are able to clothe themselves in visible physical substance.

REG —[*Aside*] Now I am able to place the rascal. [*Aloud*] I have read of you, Professor Crowell, in that extraordinary paper—" The Waving Banner of Progress."

PROF. C.—[*Walking about*] Then you know that my Materializing Circles were attended with fame and honor. The Spirit of Theodore Parker used to issue from my cabinet and dis:ourse learnedly on Biology and Mesmerism, while an Eastern Dancing Girl would move among the audience, tinkling bells and rattling castanets, with playful coquetry. Mrs. McHomery, an Irish lady, was fond of dancing to the music of our blind organist ; and our most frequent visitor—a Brave known as Red Earth—used to startle my audiences by rushing out and performing the war dance to the most blood-thrilling whoops. Drums would beat, trumpets sound, violins and tambourines float overhead, while Spirits busied themselves in materializing beautiful garments out of the common air.

EL.—[*Aside*] La ! They might have as well materialized *you* some decent clothes while they was about it.

PROF. C.—I have in one of my valises an exquisite gossamer shawl of spirit manufacture.

JUDGE.—And where were you during these manifestations Professor ?

PROF. C.—Where was I ? In my cabinet, sir ; fastened to my seat with ropes, hand-cuffs on my wrists, a plaster over my mouth, and my head tied up in a canvas bag.

JUDGE.—Humph ! that must have been deucedly unpleasant !

PROF. C.—Not in the least, my good friend. At such times I am unconscious, lost in a deep and happy trance.

REG.—[*Facing Professor*] But on one occasion—as " The Waving Banner of Progress " admitted—a light was suddenly turned on the stage, when you were discovered personating the Indian Chief.

PROF. C. -[*Grasping Reginald*] Ahem! young man, permit me to explain that little unpleasantness. On the evening in question, I was surrounded by a clique of unfriendly physicians, whose will-power. united to that of some Diakkas or Evil Spirits, overcame my will and the power of my Angel Band, and forced me on that one occasion to personate a Spirit. My enemies have made a great handle of the unfortunate occurrence to accuse me of fraud.

REG.—An ingenious explanation, truly.

PROF. C.—You doubt it, perhaps? Now see here, young man, can *you* limit the undefinable? Can *you* seek the unsearchable? Ah! truly, if we would pierce the impenetrable we must soar on the wings of the inspirational.

NI.—[*Rising*] I must remind you of the flight of time, Dr. Mann, and that I am ready to receive you and Professor Crowell elsewhere.

DR. M.—[*Rising*] Very good. Time is precious to busy folks. I lecture before the Woman's Suffrage Society in your little town, this evening. good friends, and should admire to see any of you present there.

JUDGE.—A moment of your attention, Professor. Can you make it convenient to call in upon me, say to-morrow? I should like to have you make an examination of my heart and lungs.

PROF. C.--[*Taking a bottle from valise*] Most assuredly, my good friend, most assuredly.

REG.—[*Apart*] My dear uncle, this Crowell is a rascally impostor.

JUDGE.—[*Pettishly*] Pray, mind your own business, Reginald.

NI.—We are waiting for you, Professor Crowell!

PROF. C.—One moment, Miss. [*Presenting Bottle.*] In taking my leave, Judge Erly, allow me to present you with a bottle of the Lung Healer, magnetized by Mrs. A. B. Sell.

DR. M.—And let me give you a little good advice. If you

want to make a man of yourself, quit this trick of dosing. As a witty physician has said : Pour all the medicines into the sea, and it would be a good thing for humanity, but a bad thing for the fishes.

JUDGE.—Ma'am, I want *you* to leave my house without delay.

DR. M.—[*Retiring a little up*] You should breathe the fresh air, and exercise daily.

JUDGE.—A very objectionable female! Ring the bell for Thomas, Ellen! Now, ma'am, will you leave my house?

DR. M. (R. U. C.).—Ha! ha! ha! Let's all keep our tempers. I was about to add that you must think less of yourself, Judge Erly, and more of others. Unselfishness is the best remedy for your sort of ossification of the heart.

JUDGE.—[*Rising angrily*] Clear out instantly, woman!

DR. M. (R. D.)—Ha! ha! ha! Nothing really ails you, except that you are bilious and jaundiced from laziness and gormandizing.

[JUDGE *seizes pitcher from the mantel.*]

[*Enter* THOMAS (L. D.).]

MRS. ERLY.—[*Springing up*] O Rex, Rex, don't let your uncle throw my Wedgewood pitcher!

JUDGE.—Now, woman, will you clear out?

REG.—[*Wresting pitcher from* JUDGE *and handing it to* MRS. E.] Give it to me, uncle.

MRS. E. — [*Caressing pitcher*] Such a rare specimen. Date seventeen hundred and fourteen and a genuine Flaxman design.

JUDGE.—[*Furiously*] The only thing on earth that confounded woman loves is her china. Let me get at it. [*Struggles with* REGINALD.] I'll smash the entire collection and grind the bits to powder. I'll cure her of the ceramic craze if it's my last living act. O—h! my heart, my heart. [*Stiffens back.*]

EL.—[*Aside*] La! his rage is driving him mad in earnest.

Mrs. E.—What shall we do, Rex—it's a fit?

Thomas.—Don't you fret yourself, ma'am, me and Master Reginald 'll get him into bed.

[*Exeunt* Judge, Reginald, Mrs. E., Thomas *and* Ellen, L. D.]

Dr. M. (d. c.)—Pheugh!—That's a breezy old party. Manages to keep things pretty lively here, doesn't he?

Ni.—I suppose this was intended for a business interview, Frederica, and I cannot imagine why you should have intruded yourself into the presence of my guardian and his family to disgrace me by your buffoonery.

Dr. M.—Ha! ha! ha! I couldn't resist stirring the choleric old sinner up a little, 'twill do him good! He's uglier than the theological Devil.

Ni.—I wrote requesting you to *send* Professor Crowell to me; but I'm not aware that I asked you to accompany him.

Dr. M.—No, you neglected to do so. I noticed the omission. However, it didn't matter, I had my own reasons for desiring to be present at this interview.

Ni.—Is there anything strange in it that I should desire to see the man who is to be Voltaire's companion in Europe?

Dr. M.—Nonsense! You had some other motive than a desire to *see* Confucius.

Ni.—I meant to arrange with the Professor to keep me informed of his own and his companion's movements during the next few years.

Prof. C.—And why not? Let us reason together.

Dr. M.—[*Angrily*] No doubt you're willing to betray your benefactor if you can make a good thing of it, but I object to your playing spy on Voltaire Darwin for any one's benefit.

Ni.—Hush! You need not proclaim that name in so loud a fashion. Words have wings, and we cannot always bound their flight.

Dr. M.—If I could but convince Voltaire of your villany,

Confucins, I'd soon quash this precious scheme of yours of tramping over Europe with him at his expense.

Prof. C.—No doubt your intentions are excellent, my good Dr. Mann; but, you see, Voltaire has been advised by his spirit friends.

Dr. M.—Spirit fiddle-de-dees! Talk as man to man, and don't waste twaddle on me. I can't prevent you fastening yourself on Voltaire to fatten on his fortune ; but I mean to see to it that Mistress Dare plots no new injury against him, with you for an unscrupulous tool.

Ni.—Heroics become you, Frederica; it is quite your rôle. But your infatuation for a man who never regarded your affection renders you absurdly suspicious.

Dr. M.—I'm not fool enough to expect you to understand a disinterested attachment, at all events.

[*Enter* Ellen, R. D., *carrying bottles, warming-pan, etc.*]

El. (R. U. C.).—The master is took very bad. Wants hot-water bottles, mustard plasters, warming pans, and I don't know what all. [*Crosses* L. U. C.]

[*Enter* Thomas, R. D., *carrying a bowl, etc.*]

Tho. (R. U. C.).—And a whisky-punch to make him perspire and put him to sleep.

El.—La! I wish 'twould make him sleep permanent. [*Exit* L. D.]

Ni.—Why do you disturb us ? What business have you passing through the drawing-room, Thomas ?

Tho. (L. U. C.).—'Cause, ma'am, the master wants the doctor brought to him immediate.

Ni.—[*Aside*] I must see Crowell alone. [*Aloud*] Hadn't you better go and see what can be done for Judge Erly, Dr. Mann ?

Thos.—No, ma'am ; master said he didn't want the she-doctor, but the t'other one.

Prof. C.—[*Taking up valise*] Judge Erly's a man of stupendous discernment. Fortunately I have a battery with me.

Dr. M.—[*Slapping* Professor *on shoulder*] That's right, Confucius,—manipulations spattings, and electricity will soon set the irascible old hypo on his legs again.

[*Exeunt* Prof. C. *and* Thomas (L. D.).]

Ni.—It will not surprise you to hear that I desire to see Voltaire before he leaves the country, Frederica. You must arrange for an interview.

Dr. M.—Certainly, if such is your wish. [*Aside*] I'll contrive to be present at it, however.

Ni.—And now about another matter. I have made up my mind to marry Rex Erly.

Dr. M.—More fool you! Let the boy refuse you—it's what he means to do—and you'll come into his forfeited fortune.

Ni.—But my position will be a much stronger one, if I am Mrs. Reginald Erly in the eyes of the world. But there is a girl who stands in my way.

Dr. M.—Oh, the plot thickens. I thought the amiable Rex to be invulnerable. Who is the charmer?

Ni.—Daisy Lorimer by name. A mere little nobody, poor as a nun, but beautiful as such beggars have need to be. She's a protégé of Mrs. Erly, and on a visit here. Rex is wild about her—quite ready to throw up his fortune to marry her.

Dr. M.—And what injury are you plotting her?

Ni.—None whatever. I simply want to know the *facts* of her past life. She's from Collinsville, an easy drive from here ; I want your assistance in tracing out her antecedents.

Dr. M.—I can do it, if any one can. I believe you know that I served as a detective six months of my life. It was a great success financially, you'd better believe ; but I was driven from the field by masculine jealousy.

Ni.—You see I suspect Miss Lorimer of another lover. She receives no end of illiterate scrawls to her evident annoyance. To-day, Thomas mailed a letter for her, and I took the liberty of studying the address—"Mr. William Blight, Collinsville."

Dr. M.—Blight? Euphonious patronymic that!

Ni.—If I can make Rex believe that Daisy has another lover, he will be beside himself with jealousy—the Erly temper is something fearful. If she can't deny it *in toto*, on the spot, he will listen to no excuses or explanations.

Dr. M.—Pooh! pooh! nonsense! He'd soon get over his anger, and then he'd want to hear extenuating circumstances. There'd be a few tears and not a *few* kisses, and a making-up. You can't tell me ; I know human nature.

Ni.—I should see to it that the future held no opportunities for explanations.

[*Enter* Prof. C. (L. D.).]

Prof. C. (c.).—Our honored patient is quite comfortable, ladies. I left him in the arms of sleep—balmy sleep.

Ni.—Well, nobody supposed that he was dying.

Dr. M. (R. D.).—Oh, such self-coddlers are pretty sure to live forever.

[*Exeunt* Prof. C. *and* Dr. M. (R. D.).]

Ni.—This is a dangerors game that I am playing. Reginald suspects something wrong ; but for all his boasted shrewdness I will outwit him. [*Rises.*] Daisy Lorimer shall never rule at "The Oaks," nor wear the Erly diamonds. No, Miss Daisy, go back to your obscurity, and play your humble part in life as Mrs. William Blight. [*Exit through* A.]

CURTAIN.

ACT II.

SCENE.—*Same as for Act 1. Sofa moved to* R. C.

PROPERTIES.—*A goblet and spoon on mantle. Blue dress-ing-gown ready for Thomas, right entrance.*

As curtain rises, DAISY LORIMER *is discovered seated at table* L. C.

Music plays softly during soliloquy.

DAISY.—[*Holding a letter in her hand*] What does pos-sess Billy Blight to write me so many letters? It is extreme-ly annoying. [*With excitement*] I am in a terribly false position, and all through my own fault. There is no good in denying to myself that ever since I have known Reginald Erly the very thought of Billy has been a horror to me. Dear, handsome Rex, he is my very ideal of what a lover should be!, [*Rises and walks about.*] The present state of affairs is unendurable. 1 must write to Billy and tell him *decidedly* that I would rather die than marry him. How could I ever have endured the thought? But I promised to please poor grandmamma; she was so anxious about my future. Be-sides, I didn't love any one in those days, and it was all so different. [*Examining letter.*] What a terrible scrawl Billy writes, and how frightfully ungrammatical he is. [*Reads.*] "We all of us miss you awful. Ain't you com-ing home pretty soon? Your grandma and me both think that you are making a dreadful long visit." I've half a mind to return him his letters corrected and punctuated! [*Reads.*] "I feel terrible lonesome, and am coming after you if you don't come home pretty soon." O horrors! Just imagine Billy Blight under the critical eye of Rex Erly. I wouldn't write to him at all if it were not for the fear that my silence might bring him on here. [*Reads.*] "Your grandma and me was talking about you, and she says she wishes we could get married this fall, so that she could feel you was provided for before she dies." Oh! o-h! As if I wouldn't rather scrub floors for a living! [*Throws herself on sofa, despairingly.*] I believe I fairly hate Billy Blight, and yet he isn't to blame, poor fellow! [*Starting up.*] Oh, what a wicked, wicked girl I am!

[*Enter* REGINALD *through A.*]

REGINALD (D. C.).—Fortune favors me at last! I find you alone. But why that sigh? You look as if you had lost your last friend. No bad news, I hope?

DAI.—Oh, no! only I'm cross.

REG.—*That* is news, certainly. And now, Miss Daisy, aren't you a rather small individual to monopolize the sofa? Isn't there room enough for us both?

DAI.—[*Laughing*] May be so, Mr. Erly, only I object to being crowded.

REG.—[*Seating himself beside her*] Selfish child! Do you know that you have been very cruel to me of late?

DAI.—Cruel?

REG.—You have known perfectly well that I had something serious to say to you, and yet you have denied me all opportunity for speaking to you alone.

DAI.—Oh, please do not say it.

REG.—I have been wondering how I shall endure life when you are gone, Daisy.

DAI.—You, you mean—you think—that you will miss me?

REG.—[*Taking her hand*] Fearfully! So much so that I shall soon be going after you. Shall I be welcome, Daisy dear? Don't turn your head away, but look into my eyes, like a brave little woman, and tell me if I have been a conceited fool for believing that you love me?

DAI.—[*Struggling to free herself*] No, no, of course not,

I love you dearly, with all my heart, Rex; but there is something that I must tell you.

REG.—You love me! How sweetly the confession sounds from your dear lips, Daisy. [*Places his arm about her.*] You are very young, my darling, and ignorant of the world; but I would not have it otherwise. Now I can feel certain that there has been no other lover before me. I want to be the first and the last. Why, I am of so jealous a nature, that I do not think I could ever wish to marry a girl who had once been engaged to some one else—who had ever thought of any other man as a possible husband. [DAISY *starts up excitedly.*]

DAI. (L. C.).—[*Aside*] How almost impossible he makes it for me to tell him the truth!

REG.—[*Starting up*] What is it, Daisy? Am not I the first? Answer me.

DAI.—[*Clinging to him*] The first whom I have ever loved? Oh, yes, yes, you are, indeed! But, Rex, you must listen to me.

[*The* JUDGE *is heard behind the scene, and* REGINALD *and* DAISY *start apart.*]

JUDGE.—[*Behind the scene.*] Here, Thomas, you idiot! Where the devil are you keeping yourself?

REG.—My uncle is coming. Meet me in the garden at nine this evening, sweetheart, and I will hear what you have to say, and explain to you something of the present state of my own affairs.

[DAISY *seats herself near table.*]

[*Enter* JUDGE E. (L. D.).]

JUDGE (C.).—You here, Rex, and with Miss Lorimer? Humph! Where is Nina? Where's your aunt? She knew that I was coming to the drawing-room, and that I should need a little of her attention.

[*Pulls bell-rope* L., *crosses* R., *and seats himself near fireplace.*]

Reg.—My aunt is not yet come down. [*Seats himself on sofa.*]

Judge.—I dare say not, I dare say not. Because 1 am one of that sort of people who never complain, she thinks I need no attention. No doubt she is down on her knees worshipping some monster China cat, or paying her devotion to a Florentine nautilus cup. She hasn't seen a sane moment since her great-aunt died, and left her the family bric-a-brac. Fayence, Majolica, Queen Anne tables, crocodile cups, idols, candlesticks, sconces, andirons, and the devil knows what all! I wish the Jews had the rubbish! [*Enter* Thomas l. d.] The men who invent such manias to meddle the noddles of silly women, deserve to be tied to the yard's arm, and whipped with a cat-o'-nine-tails.—Thomas, you lout!

Tho. (c.).—Yes, sir.

Judge.—This house is full of cold air.

Tho.—I don't know where it can come from, sir, for——

Judge.—How dare you to answer me back, you blockhead! [*Enter* Mrs. Ebly, l. d., *and seats herself at table near* Daisy.] If you don't know where the cold air comes from, go and find out—that's your business! I'd take my oath on a stack of Bibles as high as Babel's tower that there's a door or window open somewhere about this house. You needn't open your insolent mouth to contradict me.

[*Enter* Ellen (l. d.).]

Tho.—(l.u.c.) [*Running against* Ellen] Master's in a sweet humor.

Judge.—Is that you, Ellen?

El.—Yes, sir.

Judge.—I want to know how the mercury stands. I'll wager my head it's at the freezing point.

El.—Eighty-two, sir.

Judge.—Then some one has been breathing hot upon the thermometer to deceive me. Put it down on the floor, girl. Cold air is circulating about my feet. I wish, Rex, that you would give the carpenter orders to put up weather-strips at all the doors and windows. Mrs. Erly, can you pay me a little of your attention ?

EL.—(L. U. C.) [*Aside*] I'd like to pay you particular attention.

MRS. E.—Certainly, my dear.

JUDGE.—Then pray bear in mind the hour for my medicine, if you regard such a subject as your husband's health worthy your attention.

MRS. E.—[*Consulting watch*] I have not forgotten it, my dear.

JUDGE.—Humph! I never dare rely over much on your memory. No doubt, it ought to be a woman's greatest happiness to minister to the wants of an invalid husband; but you prefer to fiddle-faddle your time away on gew-gaws and gim-cracks. An interesting companion for an intellectual man, truly.

EL.—(L. U. C.). [*Aside*] La! what a command of language he's got. [*Enter* THOMAS *first, and* DR. MANN *second* (R. D.).] La! The self-made man again.

THO. (R. U. C.).—Dr. Mann to see Miss Dare.

MRS. E.—You may inform Miss Dare, Thomas. She is not yet down.

[*Exit* THOMAS (L. D.).]

JUDGE.—It was but yesterday that I ordered you from my house, Dr. Mann.

DR. M.—[*Seating herself* (L. U. C.).] Oh, that's all right! I took no offence ; I'm not one of the sort of folks who expect to be made a great fuss over.

JUDGE.—[*Aside*] An outrageous young woman! [*Aloud*] Ellen, ring the bell for Thomas. Mrs. Erly, you are forgetting the hour for my medicine.

MRS. E.—[*Consulting watch*] It still lacks a few minutes of the time, my dear. Ellen, hand the Judge the goblet from the mantel. [*Ellen crosses* (R.).]

JUDGE.—Humph! You would have forgotten had not I reminded you. [*Taking goblet from Ellen and sipping medicine.*] Here, take the glass, you cat, and clear out! [*Enter* THOMAS, L. D.]

DR. M.—[*Aside*] Aggravating old party! I'd admire to give him a caning!

JUDGE.—I want my blue dressing-gown, dunder pate! [*Exit* THOMAS (L. D.).] As I cannot regulate the matter of heat in this house, I am obliged to accommodate myself to changes of temperature by varying the number of my garments. At this very moment I have on three waistcoats and two dressing-gowns.

DR. M.—Ha! ha! ha! A delightful bulbo-tuber arrangement. You can then peel yourself like an onion.

JUDGE.—Woman!

DR. M.—Let's all keep our tempers! One of the little jokes I must have. Very bad habit of mine, joking, I confess.

JUDGE.—[*Aside*] Humph! A most objectionable female! [*Aloud*] Ellen, the fire is dying out.

EL.—[*Aside*] I wish you was! [*Appears to stir the fire.*]

[*Enter* THOMAS (L. D.).]

THO. (C.)—The blue dressing-gown, sir. Will you have it on?

JUDGE.—Would you kill me, you murdering hound? I'll wager my neck you've just taken it out of some cursed damp hole of a closet. Hang it up before the fire. [THOMAS *hangs it over the back of a chair before fire. Exit* THOMAS R. D.]

EL.—[*Aside*] Oh la! what an old fuss. [*Takes a fan from mantel and waves it slyly.*]

JUDGE.—Aha! I'm certain that I feel cold air stirring. I'm not to be deceived. My blood is as sensitive as mercury.

[*Enter* THOMAS *first, and* PROFESSOR CROWELL *second,* R. D.]

THO. (R. U. C.)--Professor Confucius Crowell. [*Exit* R. D.]

PROF. C. (C.)--Beloved friends, I come into your midst breathing the sweet influences of my Medicine Band. Let us enter together the Pantheon of Progress. We must soar on the wings of the inspirational if we would pierce the impenetrable.

[*Exit* ELLEN, L. D.]

REG.—[*Apart*] I know this man to be a wretched charlatan who has been indicted more than once for malpractice. I trust you will give up the idea of consulting him professionally, my dear uncle.

JUDGE.--Oh, you're like all the others, Rex. You think because I never complain that nothing really ails me. Now I am convinced that Professor Crowell, being a clairvoyant, will be able to tell me the causes of my great physical sufferings.

DR. M.--[*Walking about*] No doubt about it, no doubt whatever! By the way, Crowell, did I ever tell you of my little experience with the Spiritualists? I fell in with some of them at Buffalo and developed myself as a Medium. Financially it was a great success. My specialty was taking casts of spirit hands. But one day luck changed. A paraffine mould tumbled out of my bag rather inopportunely, and I had some trouble in getting out of the small town I was in without a *wumpus* and a *woir*.

REG.—If I understand you, Dr. Mann, you confess yourself and Professor Crowell to be a pair of rascally swindlers.

DR. M.--Oh, a joke, Erly! I must have my little jokes.

PROF. C.—My Medicine Band, Judge Erly, is composed of several Spirits. Under the control of the Ex-Rev. Dr. Windmere Rush, I am able to give psychometrical delineations of character. The true physician studies the mind as well as the body.

DR. M.--That's a sound doctrine. Mind is but a secretion of matter. There's no such thing as a soul among your advanced thinkers. Give the brain of your idiot deeper channelling, put in more phosphorus, and perhaps a pinch of sulphur, and you've got a Shakspeare. Or let the molecules take new shapes and currents of motion in the head of a villain and you've got a saint.

PROF. C.--In reading physical conditions, Judge Erly, I am inspired by the Spirit of the late Dr. Alonzo Ottenheimer. Ever since his translation he has been a pupil of Esculapius, who now presides over a Medical College in the Island Delphina. Through him I am a diagnostical clairvoyant. But I am not limited to the descriptional, I have also the prescriptional power. Without vanity, I may call myself the Many Gifted. As a remedial physician, I am governed by the Spirit of my Bride—the Beatified Aurelia. She has become deeply skilled in the nature of herb and vegetable properties under the tuition her Indian attendant, Little-Blue-Corn-Flower.

JUDGE.--I think we'd better proceed to the clairvoyant examination of my physical condition, Professor, if you are ready to pay me your attention.

PROF. C.—[*Seating himself in front of* JUDGE] Let us seat ourselves, then, in philosophical harmony with the polarities of the magnetic principle. As I take your right hand in my left, so our vital mental spheres are attracted toward each other. Will you oblige me, Dr. Mann, by reporting the diagnosis the late Dr. Alonzo Ottenheimer will, no doubt, soon enable me to give?

DR. M. (R.)—[*Tipping her chair back and taking out note-book and pencil*] Certainly, certainly ; anything to oblige.

[*Pause during which* PROFESSOR CROWELL *appears to be entranced.*]

PROF. C.—The Ex-Rev. Dr. Windmere Rush desires to utter an invocation.

REG.—My dear uncle, this is being carried too far ; I beg of you to interfere.

JUDGE.—[*Testily*] And I beg of you not to interfere.

PROF. C.—We invoke the Force that we find in the Mineral, Animal, and Vegetable Kingdoms. We petition that the teachers of orthodoxy may be shown that they are more ignorant than the Heathen whom they profess to enlighten. We beseech our Spirit Friends here present to accept our thoughts and carry them along the Milky Way. And now let us so elevate our souls that our electric current may be formed upon which their thoughts can be transmitted to us in return.

DR. M.—[*With mock solemnity*] Second the motion.

PROF. C.—O wonderful Spirit of Harmony! the magnetic circles now blend. I behold a human organism clairvoyantly, and am able to analyze all that is abnormal. The processes of the *endosmosis* and the *exosmosis* are not in a balanced condition. [DR. MANN *begins to write.*] There is something wrong in the empire of the *ganglionic* jurisdiction. I see disease of the *medulla oblongata*. The *pneumognostic* nerves are disturbed, and a shadow lies about the *cordiac plexus*. Alas! that faithful shadow indicates heart-disease. Now I behold the heart clearly. It is covered with calcareous excrescences which absolutely impinge on the lungs. [*With fearful contortions*] The occult law of sympathy begins to work. I feel with another's consciousness. I can no longer remain under this control—my sensations are too horrible! My heart palpitates; my throat burns; I itch, and am too feeble to scratch; my hands and feet are cold as in death; and my soul is overwhelmed with dark forebodings. Oh! oh-h! [*Comes out of trance and appears to wipe perspiration from his brow.*]

JUDGE.—Now this is amazing, supernatural! Professor Crowell has experienced my very sensations.

DR. M.—[*Rising*] Here is the diagnosis, Crowell. [*Hands paper.*]

PROF. C.—I will consult with my beatified Aurelia as to

the advisable remedies, when next I am in my superior state. [*Throws himself upon sofa as if greatly exhausted.*]

DR. M.—[*Takes out note-book.*] The symptoms seem to me very alarming, Judge Erly ; it's my honest opinion that you have but a few months to live. If you can pay me a little of your attention, here is a matter that will interest you. I have in this book the names of a number of persons who desire to be cremated after death. With the Ancients it was a favorite method of disposing of the human remains : no doubt it is the cleanly, the sanitary——

JUDGE.—Woman, if you don't want to be kicked out of my house——

DR. M.—[*Putting away note-book and taking out another*] Oh, no offence ! Some people have an unreasonable prejudice against cremation, I know. Now I represent the Boston Woman's Medical Society. We are in need of a few first-class skeletons. Will us your body and I'll promise to articulate you with my own hands. I'll turn you out beautifully white and small ; you'll never complain, and I'll warrant that the job will give entire satisfaction to your friends.

JUDGE.- Ma'am, you're the most outrageous woman I've ever met!

DR. M.—Ha! ha! ha! Let's all keep our tempers! A joke, of course ; I must have my little jokes. [PROFESSOR *takes books from valise and puts them on table. Enter* NINA (L. D.).]

JUDGE.—[*Rising*] I disapprove of you utterly, ma'am. I consider you a very improper acquaintance for my ward, Miss Dare. I may be behind the times, but in my opinion a virtuous young woman should be modest in her dress, and quiet in her manners.

DR. M.—Ha! ha! ha! Old fogyism on the rampage! You'll live to be woman-dozed, Judge Erly. Give woman suffrage, and the ballot will soon right her ancient wrongs. The tyrant man must take a back seat. His is the brute force eventually to be controlled and utilized by the higher intelligence.

JUDGE.—[*Sinking down on sofa*] The higher intelligence! Hear the woman! She's an escaped lunatic! Oh, oh—h! my poor, fluttering heart!

PROF. C.—[*To* DAISY] I'd like to tell this young lady's fortune. For a trifling fee of five dollars I can cast her horoscope after the methods of the most ancient and learned astrologers.

REG.—You needn't address yourself to that young lady, sir.

PROF. C.—[*Spreading books out on table*] Perhaps the ladies would like to examine some books I have with me to-day?

REG.—So, you're a book agent, after all?

PROF. C.—Only in the cause of truth, my friends, only in the cause of truth.

[*Enter* THOMAS (R. D.).]

NI.—I believe you called to see *me*, Dr. Mann.

DR. M.—Oh! good day, Nina, good day!

THO. (C.)—A peddler at the door, Mrs. Erly, says you've promised to look at some red and gold cups and sassers.

MRS. E.—[*Rising*] Ask him to the dining-room, Thomas. [*Exit* THOMAS (L. D.).] It's the Kaga ware I was telling you about, my dear Daisy, and with the mark " Kutani."

[DAISY *rises and* NINA *seats herself at table.*]

JUDGE.—Don't you invest a red cent in it, Mrs. Erly; it's only a month since you spent a small fortune on a plate.

MRS. E.—But such a rare specimen, my dear—a genuine Ravenna, dated fifteen hundred and eighty-two.

PROF. C.—But the books, ladies, the books!

MRS. E.—Not to-day. I confess that I am more interested in china than in books.

PROF. C.—No doubt, China is immensely interesting, ma'am; I myself was named for the greatest sage of that favored clime. [*Shoves books aside, takes out planchette, and appears to write rapidly during following conversation.*]

Dr. M.—One moment, ladies! Examine these circulars. [*Hands circulars.*] You see, I'm agent for the reform clothing; I'm in for reforms of all sorts, civil and uncivil. Leave off your murderous stays and heavy, dragging skirts, my friends, and order the Progressive Health Costumes from this Boston firm; you'll gain years of life by the operation.

Mrs. E.—We do not contemplate making any decided changes in our mode of dress at present, Dr. Mann; your occupations seem to be numerous.

Dr. M.—You may well say so, my good woman. I've tried a little of most everything, and not always with financial success. Now there was blue glass, for instance; craze died out just as I had a lot of the brittle stuff on hand. Then there was the New Harmonical Community; I went on intending to join, but found the members to be poor, limited creatures, with no breadth of horizon, and was glad enough to cut and run. I went into co-operative housekeeping with a set that vamoosed, leaving the concern disgracefully in debt. Ever since I can remember I've been a sort of nine-pin for fate—no sooner set up than bowled down again. [*Exeunt Mrs. E. and Daisy through* A.] (D. C.) But I am one of that sort of people who never complain. [*Taking out cigar-case.*] Have a cigar, Erly?— fine brand.

Reg.—Thank you, no.

Judge.—[*Aside*] A most objectionable young woman.

Dr. M.—[*Pushing chair aside, standing with back to fire, striking a match on sole of her boot, and lighting a cigar.*] I'm a genuine believer in the weed myself. A great deal of nervous irritability goes off in smoke.

Prof. C.—Judge Erly, you are probably aware that Spiritualism has a large and distinctive literature of its own, that stands like a pyramid of solidity amid the weak trash of the day. Here is the "Divine Arcana," for instance, a book with idees enough to revolutionize this globe. • Here is "A Wail from the Pews," by A. J. Tator; it has shaken Bigotry on its throne. Here is "Old Theology Turned Wrong Side Out," by Mrs. Cockburn Crow. *You'd* better buy a copy, young man. Now were I a Bloated Aristocrat, or one of your Bond-holding Rothschilds, I'd *present* you with one— and why? Because I pity you, sir. Your mind is a fossil, a relic of the middle ages, a nineteenth-century anachronism. A book like this would expand your horizon and enlarge your narrer views. Or buy "Orthodoxy Unveiled," by that great Revelator, Mrs. Wurtzel Buzzard.

REG.—Your books are not to my taste.

PROF. C.—Now see here, young man, we can't all be Wurtzel Buzzards, Tappings, Hyzers, Hawks or Cockburn Crows; but at least we need not shut ourselves up in casings of learned ignorance and refuse to receive true knowledge.

NI.—[*Aside*] How shall I contrive to see Professor Crowell alone? [*Appears to write on a slip of paper.*]

REG.—You'd better repack your books; no one here patronizes that sort of literature.

PROF. C.—Aha! young man. I read you. You are afraid of these New Lights! You prefer to walk by conservative tallow dips all your life! Am I obscure?

JUDGE —[*Rising*] Lend me your arm, Rex. [REG. *rises and assists* JUDGE] I am now ready for an electrical treatment, Professor, if you can pay me a little of your attention. My animal magnetism is always at its best at this hour.

PROF. C.—Very well, Judge Erly, very well! But won't you buy one or two of these books?

JUDGE.—Yes, yes, certainly, leave a copy of each. [NINA *makes a sign to attract* PROFESSOR CROWELL'S *attention.*]

PROF. C.—May they be a blessing to you and an assistance in your noble search for truth. And now you must buy my patent planchette with mediometer. It is simply invaluable if you desire to develop yourself as a medium.

JUDGE.—Yes, yes, leave it, leave it, by all means.

PROF. C.—[*Crossing to* NINA, *spreading photographs before her, and receiving a slip of paper*] Perhaps this young lady would like to examine some spirit photographs? Here are several of Katy King, taken in London by aid of a magnesium lamp. A Grecian Princess, an Indian——

NI.—[*Scornfully*] Oh, I'm not interested in such rubbish!

JUDGE.—[*Testily*] If you can't pay *me* a little of your attention, Professor Crowell——

PROF. C.—[*Packing valise*] Certainly, certainly, I and my blessed Medicine Band are now at your service.

[*Exeunt* JUDGE E. *and* REGINALD, *followed by* PROFESSOR C. (L. D.).]

DR. M.—[*Crossing to* NINA] Well, I've interviewed Voltaire, Mistress Dare. He will be in the garden at a little past eight this evening. Can you contrive to slip out unobserved?

NI.—Oh, yes, without difficulty.

DR. M.—And no tricks, mind, or I'll be on your track. Voltaire is a frail, sickly creature, all imagination and nerves. No match for an unscrupulous, desperate woman, and a professional knave. Poor fellow! he needs a friend.

NI.—Well, and you're welcome to be as much his friend as ever you choose, Fred. And now about Daisy Lorimer. You've not had time to make inquiries as yet, I suppose?

DR. M.—Haven't I? Well, I'm just back from Collinsville, and I shan't meddle if you play the innocent Daisy a trick or two.

NI.—What do you mean?

DR. M.—[*Walking about*] I mean that she's one of those unprincipled little wretches who think it no harm to pain an honest heart if it happens to beat under a bumpkin's jacket.

NI.—I don't understand.

Dr. M. — Why, this Mildew—this Blight—this what's-his-name! Miss Daisy left Collinsville engaged to him.

Ni.—Actually engaged? That is better than I dared hope.

Dr. M.—I gained admission to the tumble-down shanty in my professional character, and interviewed the grandmother who is on her last legs. Found her garrulous and confiding, after the nature of simple old women. She informed me where Daisy was visiting, and that, upon her return home, she was to be married to their young neighbor, Mr. William Blight. Ny doubt you'll understand how to play this card. And now I must be off. My baggage is at the door, and my horse restless. I have to drive over to the Woman's Dialectical Club, where there's a debate pending. Ta! ta! [*Exit* B. D.]

Ni. --I must gain a solemn promise from Voltaire that he will not expose my past history. Why should he? He has nothing to gain by ruining me, unless he should see too much of Frederica, who worships him, when legal freedom might become of consequence to him. [*Rises*] It is well that he is to leave America, and with this wretch, Crowell. 1 am not safe while Voltaire lives. And now for an opportunity of interviewing Rex, after which his mood will be a very tender one when next he meets with you, Daisy Lorimer. Ha! ha! ha! [*Exit through* A.]

CURTAIN.

ACT III.

SCENE. —*A garden at " The Oaks ;" large window, with marble steps leading from it at rear. Three large vases (practicable) with flowers* (L.) *; trees and entrances* (R.) *; garden bench* (R).

Enter JUDGE ERLY *and* PROFESSOR CROWELL *through window.*

PROF. C. (D. C.).—[*Supporting* JUDGE] Spiritualism, my dear Judge Erly, is the perfected blossom of our nineteenth century civilization. Many of our best and greatest thinkers are now avowed believers.

JUDGE.—And many others, like myself, are earnest investigators. Nothing but my deep interest in the search for truth could have induced me to venture forth to breathe the malarial poison of the night air. [*Coughs*] I'm an Æolian harp, painfully susceptible to the loud noises and rough shocks of the world in which I live.

PROF. C.—And has it never struck you, my dear friend, that the spirits might be able to evolve rare harmonies from so finely strung an instrument? Come, let us reason together.

JUDGE.—Ahem! You mean, perhaps, that I may be an undeveloped medium, or sensitive?

PROF. C.—And why not? I think it highly· probable. We can determine the matter by means of a clairvoyant examination ; for I find that medianimic gifts depend very much upon parts about the *corpus callosum* and those· above the *corpora striata.*

JUDGE.—We must have an examination then––say, tomorrow. And now, if you can pay me a little of—that is, if you please—we'll proceed to the cosmographic exposition.

PROF. C.—One moment, Judge Erly, I desire to improve this opportunity for private speech, by mentioning to you a somewhat startling circumstance. You remember that yesterday I beheld the spirit of a beautiful woman in robes of transcendental whiteness, hovering above your head?

JUDGE—Ahem! I remember—certainly.

PROF. C.--She appeared to me again in a vision of the night.

JUDGE.--Strange!

PROF. C.—She expressed a desire. Judge Erly, that you and me should arrange for a Cabinet Séance, when she says she will attempt to materialize. If successful, she wants you should hold yourself in readiness to be married to her.

JUDGE.--The devil! You forget Mrs. Erly.

PROF. C.—Let us reason together, my dear friend. With the keen eye of the Inspired Seer, I have observed that your good and amiable lady is not your Soul's Affinity.

JUDGE.--Humph! Of course, she isn't; but that's no reason why I should put her away. From what I have seen, I should say that very few people *are* united to their affinities.

PROF. C.- Very true, and it is to right the mistakes of planetary existence that marriages are hourly celebrated in the First and Second Spheres of the Summer Land. But why procrastinate, when, without injury to any. we may enjoy the high delights of spiritual converse with Kindred Souls while still in this mundane state?

[*Enter* REGINALD *through* w.]

REGINALD (R. U. C.).—[*Aside*] As I live, my uncle, and with that inspirational old rascal who has gained such an influence over him!

PROF. C.--[*Unrolling a picture and afterwards placing his valises under the bench*] My Spirit Bride, the Beatified Aurelia, was on earth the wife of the Medium Slate, justly celebrated for his reading of folded pellets. Shortly after her translation, Aurelia materialized, and was married to me in the presence of witnesses.

Judge.—And didn't Slate object ?

Prof. C.—Certainly not ; why should he have ? Let us reason together. Slate is a man who has great breadth of horizon—his ideas and mine are very similar. Besides, he is now united to his own affinity, Joan D'Arc, known in history as the Maid of Orleans. Joan and Aurelia are now waiting for Slate and I on the planet Herschel, which they describe as unsuited to human existence. Eventually we shall all start together for the bright Zone in the region of Cygnus the Swan. [*Holding up picture*] Beatific Aurelia, I behold thee !

Judge.—That's a wonderful picture !

Reg.—[*Aside*] What deviltry is the old sinner concocting now ?

Prof. C.—Wonderful indeed ! Let us draw near to the light and study these supermundane charms. [Judge *and* Professor *move* U. C. Reginald *down stage to* 2 v. l.]. In such heavenly guise did my Beatified Aurelia reveal herself to Sister Tapping of Revelation Vale, who sketched this picture with bandaged eyes while in a state of trance. It represents my Angel-Love star-crowned and with floating hair, as you see, hovering above the Pyramids of Egypt, gathering wisdom from the Fount of the Ancients.

Judge (D. C.).—And you advise my entering into one of these spiritual unions ?—I don't know that it would be expedient.

Prof. C.—[*Replacing picture in valise and taking out map*] And why not ? Surely your spirit is in advance of the age in which you live ! You are one of those who have entered the Pantheon of Progress. Is not your soul unmated ? Are not you lonely in a universe full of love ? Follow a new Light—be ecstatic and rejoice ! No doubt your spirit's mate will select a medium through whom she can communicate to you her wishes ; she will thus become, though all unseen, the guiding star of your existence. I trust that I am not obscure.

REG.—[*Approaching*] You are a villain, and I trust that my uncle will not insult his family by putting himself in the equivocal position your proposition implies.

JUDGE.—Ahem! You here, Rex?

PROF. C.—Aha! young man, I read you, ubiquitous and obreptitious as you seem to be. You are without any far-reaching aspiration towards the super-mundane. Your true belief of the Spirits is that they are helplessly bottled up, waiting for the sound of a hypothetical trumpet. [*Grasping* REGINALD *excitedly*] Throw off the dark robes of Bigotry and clothe yourself in the rich garments of Free and Progressive Thought! An opportunity now offers for you to learn Eternal Truth! Listen with a candid mind while I reveal to you my Plan of the Universe. [*Unrolls map.*]

REG.—If your utterances are not blasphemy, they are the ravings of a lunatic.

PROF. C.—I resent the charge of lunacy, and fling it back in the face of him who utters it. Know, sir, that I am acknowledged Thought-Leader, the President of the Advance Guard Theosophical Society of Boston, whose learned discussions are far beyond the comprehension of the limited individual whom I am now addressing.

REG.—Humph! That may or may not be.

JUDGE (U. C.).—This damp, malarial night-air is chilling me to the marrow, Professor, so if you cannot pay me a little of your attention——

PROF. C.—[*Grasping* JUDGE] Certainly, certainly. certainly, my good friend, let us proceed!—No doubt this young man has been brought up to reverence the ignorant and bigoted Milton, who, living in an age when the Copernican Philosophy was accepted by all learned astronomers, preferred to cling to the rotten Ptolemaic System! Let us reason together without fear and without favor. John Milton had the false, I have the true Cosmogony of the Universe. Again and again has my soul been transported to many of the places I am about to describe. It is a fact that by respiring internally I am able to breathe the air of three spheres without loss of consciousness, and can therefore move at will in the Angelic Societies of the Celestial and Ultimate Degrees.

REG.—Absurd!

PROF. C.—[*Pointing*] Gaze up into the east, gentlemen, and behold the Pleiades! Brightest of the seven Sisters behold Alcyone! Can it be denied that she is the centre of our planetary system? Nay, it cannot, for so it has been revealed. Alcyone, mother of the Sun, is grandmother to the Earth. Can it be denied, then, that she is great-grandmother to the Moon? Am I obscure, or are ye, my hearers, obtuse? Your thoughts appear to wander, young man.

REG.—I am listening to your learned dissertation with as much attention as it deserves.

PROF. C.—I read you, sir! You doubt my being a seer? Let us reason together. I was the child of poor and dishonest parents. When but nine of years age, they died. I was made into a common drudge. I never received a day's schooling in my life, nor was so much as taught wherein one letter of the alphabet differeth from another. [*Enter* ELLEN *through* w.] If the Invisibles have not rescued me and taught me through Interior Communion, how do you account for the learning I possess on every conceivable subject?

ELLEN (D. C.).—The silver spoons is gone from the sideboard, Judge Erly, a whole lot of 'em——

JUDGE.—Humph! the devil! Was ever a gentleman so tormented with careless, dishonest servants?

REG.—If Professor Crowell will stand to one side and permit me to examine those valises, I think I shall be able to produce the lost silver.

PROF. C.—I'll permit nothing of the sort, you Purse-proud young Aristocrat! Do you imagine that, because I am not one of your Bloated, Bond-holding Rothschilds, I'm to be insulted with impunity?

REG.—[*Drawing a revolver*] I intend inspecting the contents of those valises whether you object or not.

JUDGE.—Nonsense, Rex, you are always suspecting the most unlikely people! [*Sinking upon garden bench*] Oh, my heart, my poor fluttering heart! Such a scene is too much for my shattered nerves!

PROF. C.—[*Moving aside*] No violence, young man, no violence, I implore! The Innocent Victim of Unjust Suspicion submits to Superior Force!

ELLEN—[*Dragging the valises out and opening them*] Ha! ha! ha! You just keep that persuader pointed, Mr. Erly, and I'll search his valises.

PROF. C.—[*Gazing upward*] Yes, I behold thee, Beatific Aurelia—I hear thy Pleading Voice! For thy sake, I will be patient with the Ruthless Insultor, conscious that my Innocence will soon shine forth radiant as the Unsullied Sun to overwhelm with deserved shame the Rash Accuser.

EL.—Here they be, Mr. Erly, sure as you live! One, two, three, four, six, eight, ten, twelve of the big ones—and six of the little gold-lined ones.

REG.—Is that correct?

EL.—Yes, sir, that's just what we mis ed. [*Exit through* w.]

REG.—This is a very serious matter, Professor Crowell. [*Seizing him by the collar.*] Possibly you can explain it.

PROF. C.—Most assuredly I can, young man, most assuredly I can. Permit me to say, however, that your suspiciousness has caused me the deepest pain. Now I recognize in this a malicious trick of a Diakka. At a late Séance there issued from my Cabinet the dusky, dark, undeveloped spirit of an African Idiot, who behaved so outrageously that my Angel Band were obliged to handle him rather roughly. He vanished, swearing revenge, and has no doubt availed himself of this opportunity to injure me.

REG.—[*Shaking the* PROF. *fiercely.*] Say the word, uncle, and I'll kick this rascal out of the grounds!

JUDGE.—Don't be a fool, Rex! [*Rising*] I desire you, to release your hold on Professor Crowell at once. Had you read up on this subject, you would know that such cases are of frequent occurrence, and that the explanation you have just listened to is undoubtedly the true one. *I* consider it perfectly satisfactory.

PROF. C.—I thank you for your generous confidence, my noble friend! Nevertheless I am grieved and alarmed at this occurrence, knowing, as I do, that the Demon Diakkas could never have thus approached and controlled me had not some malign influence temporarily weakened the power of my Angel Band.

JUDGE.—Say no more. We will dismiss this painful theme, and go on with the discussion of your inspired cosmography.

PROF. C.—Very well, excellent friend, so let it be. We will leave the Pleiades, as only a few unique and daring Spirits from our Earth have ever started on that long and awful journey. [*Pointing*] Gaze up into the Milky Way, gentlemen, and behold the Heaven of your dreams! Probably this young man is not able to trace Perseus in the Heavens. But look here upon my map. [*Grasping Reginald*] Here in the region of Perseus you see an oval outline. It marks the site of the egg-shaped Island of Supreme Delight. Where you behold this red dot stands the fairy Temple Glenderosiphina, with its billions of cupolas, minarets, domes and towers of ivory, pearl and gold. A rainbow of dazzling light spans the Island, while comets of amazing size further illumine its skies.

[*Enter* NINA *through* W.]

NINA (R. U. C.)—[*Aside*] I must contrive to get these people in from the garden.

PROF. C.—On the golden steps of Glenderosiphina I

have frequently heard the Spirit Lady, Nambypabuluma, instructing children from our own and other planets.

Nɪ. (ᴅ. ᴄ.)—I am surprised to find you in the open air studying the stars, Judge Erly.

Jᴜᴅɢᴇ.—Humph! the devil! It seems I cannot move without being followed by every member of my family.

Nɪ. —Oh ! I was in search of Rex.

Pʀᴏꜰ. C.—[*Grasping* Nɪɴᴀ] This blue line, Miss, marks the site of Airy Nella. Through this land of milk and honey flows the Lulabylatrula. You will reach its banks, my beloved hearers, in precisely one hour and twenty minutes after quittation of the body. [*Grasping* Rᴇɢɪɴᴀʟᴅ *excitedly*] The music of the sweet Spring Murmurilla will first greet your ears. You will pluck the Gardenympha and other Spirit Flowers. You will listen enchanted to the bird songs of the Tristella from Saturn, the Bulbul from Earth, and the Violiola from Venus.

Rᴇɢ.—[*Freeing himself*] Enough of this rubbish! And don't lay hands on me again unless you want a kicking. [*Appears to converse with* Nɪɴᴀ (ʟ. ᴜ. ᴏ.).]

Pʀᴏꜰ. C.—Poor misguided young man ! His mind now is shut up in a six-foot thick wall of Bigotry. But these idees of mine have startled skeptics before now, and hit Orthodoxy some telling blows (ᴜ. ᴄ). Ah ! truly, my friend, if we would pierce the impenetrable, we must soar on the wings of the inspirational.

[*Exeunt* Pʀᴏꜰ. *and* Jᴜᴅɢᴇ *through* ᴡ.]

Rᴇɢ. (ʟ. ᴄ.). —Be brief, Nina, if that which you have to say concerns my relations with Miss Lorimer.

Nɪ. (ᴄ.).—I can be very brief, if you desire. I have only to tell you that I have been informed that Daisy Lorimer came here an engaged girl; that she is to be married upon her return to Collinsville to one Mr. William Blight. Tax her with it, and see if she will deny it. [*Retires* (ᴜ. ᴏ.).]

Reg.—[*Fiercely*] It is false, idle gossip! Who was your informant?

Ni.—Don't be so absurdly tragical! My informant was Dr. Frederica Mann, who simply repeated to me what she heard on all sides. Miss Lorimer is the proper person for you to question and brow-beat, not I. [*Exit through* w.]

Reg.—Great Heaven! I will get at the bottom of this miserable business. [*Exit through* w.]

[*Enter* Dr. Mann, r. 2 e.]

Dr. Mann (c.).—There's a wind abroad that means mischief, and I alone seem conscious of its stirrings. I must witness this interview between Nina and Voltaire, for I may be able to unravel her schemes where he'd see only innocent intention. I haven't a doubt she means to use Crowell as her tool, but it's quite impossible to put Voltaire on his guard against that old rascal, for he believes in all his absurd pretensions. What a misfortune it is to be over-credulous!

[*Enter* Voltaire Darwin (r. 1 e.).]

Voltaire.—I'm surprised to find *you* here, Frederica. Where is Nina? Has she consent.d to your being present at our interview?

Dr. M.—I haven't asked her consent. Probably she hasn't been able to give her lynx-eyed guardian the slip as yet.

Vol.—My soul revolts at the thought of a meeting with her, Frederica; I wish that it could be avoided.

Dr. M.—Nonsense! Why should you dread meeting her? I'll wager my head, her desire to see you is founded on nothing more than a fear that you have betrayed her secret.

Vol.—Why should she doubt my honor?

Dr. M.—'Tis not a question of honor. Prof. Crowell certainly knows something, and——

Vol.—He has learned nothing from me, Frederica. Of course, I can't say what he knows, as many things are revealed to him supernaturally.

Dr. M.—I wish that I could convince you what a rascal this Crowell really is.

Vol.—But how can *you* judge him fairly, Frederica? You deny the possibility of supernatural gifts, even of spiritual existence.

Dr. M.—Of course I do! We're curious bits of protoplasm, rare machines kept in motion by supplies of food and drink, and when we run down there's an end of it.

Vol.—Why do you not accuse me of being a fraud as well as Professor Crowell, since I too claim to be a medium, though with lesser gifts?

Dr. M.—Oh, there are mediums *and* mediums! You are genuine enough, as mediums go. I divide them into two classes—those who are a little *non compos mentis*, believers in their own sickly hallucinations, and those who are simply impostors. In my opinion the cheats have the best of it, for they are quite as successful financially, and they don't suffer from a drain upon the nervous system.

Vol.—I cannot accept your conclusions, Frederica; I do not simply believe; I have absolute knowledge of the truth of spiritual existence. The more I meditate, aspire, and mortify the flesh, the more wonderful grow the phenomena produced through my medinmship. It has often been accorded me to behold the spirit forms of departed friends when in ecstasy or trance.

Dr. M.—Such hallucinations are the premonitions of insanity, Voltaire; I warn you as a physician.

Vol.— I saw my father's spirit on the night of his death, Frederica.

Dr. M.—You believed that you did, Voltaire. The truth is, you are surrounded by a dominant, all-pervading thought atmosphere. The rest is mere coincidence. [*Crosses* L.] 'Tis rather singular that the child of parents who believed next to nothing should be so very credulous. But there's no use in arguing with you, for you're incorrigible—Nina's coming! I'll just squirm behind this pot of posies, and hear what she has to say for herself. [*Steps behind* 2 v.] Don't you betray me : 'tis one of the little jokes I must have.

[*Enter* NINA DARE *through* w.]

NINA (D. C.).—You here, Voltaire! I will detain you but a moment, as I fear discovery. I requested this interview because I wanted to hear from your own lips, and not through Frederica Mann, that you don't object to my disposing of myself and of my property as I see fit.

VOL.—Why should I object? Five years ago I told you to go your way, as I should go mine. Our union was a horror, and we dissolved it. It was my awful misfortune, when in a clairvoyant state, to see into your soul and read its dark designs, till you became to me a terror and a shame.

NI.—Was not there something to be said on my side? What woman would like for a husband a diseased, uncanny creature, endowed with the undesirable power of reading her secret thoughts? I confess that I have a horror of the abnormal.

VOL.—Let us indulge in no more of these useless recriminations. You have nothing to fear from me, Nina. I am about to leave the country for an indefinite time, and do not desire to interfere with your future in any way.

NI.—Is my secret safe, Voltaire?

VOL.—And why not? It is known but to ourselves, to Frederica, and to an obscure country dominie who has doubtless long since forgotten our names and faces.

NI.—Is it safe with Frederica? She adores *you*, and should you ever take a notion to honor her with your love in return, she would want you to sue me for a divorce.

VOL.—This is worse than folly! You insult an innocent woman who is my friend.

NI.—Ah, well, I am not here to discuss Frederica Mann; there is some one else I want to know about—this Professor Crowell. Who is he? Where did you make his acquaintance?

Vol.—I was introduced to him by the spirit friends who have advised my asking him to accompany me to Europe.

Ni.—Introduced by spirit friends! I do not know that I understand you.

Vol.—I consult them by means of sealed letters sent to Sister Tapping, of Revelation Vale, and receive answer through their mediumship.

Ni.—And the letters you write?

Vol.—Are returned to me intact, with seals unbroken. If you have no further explanations to demand, we will not prolong this interview, for I find it extremely trying to my nerves.

Ni.—There is nothing more—unless——

Vol.—Then I will leave you, and I trust that we shall never meet again. [*Exit* R. 1 E.]

Ni.—Poor, credulous fool! It is well this precious Revelation Vale correspondence through the inspired Sister Tapping is manipulated by Professor Crowell, whose interests must be identified with my own. (L.) But here comes Daisy Lorimer, no doubt for a sentimental meeting with Rex. [*Steps behind* 1 v.] I must watch the play of the elements I have set in motion.

[*Enter* Daisy Lorimer *through* w. *Music plays softly.*]

Dai. (D. C.)—No one here? I must chide Rex for letting me be the first at the rendezvous. [*Crosses* R. *and seats herself on garden bench.*] I need a moment in which to gather up my courage for confession. I have been weak and wicked, but surely he will forgive me. [Reginald Erly *appears in* w.] Ah! there he is, dear, handsome Rex, but he does not see me! [*Rises and advances to* C. Reginald *approaches to within a short distance of* Daisy, *and pauses with folded arms.*] How strangely you look at me, Rex! What is the matter? Why do you not speak?

Reg.—[*Fiercely*] When I speak it will be to curse you!

Dai.—Oh, no, no; not that!

Reg.—To utter words of hatred and contempt.

Dai.—What do you mean ?

Reg.—Are you the pure and innocent girl whom I have so loved and trusted ?

Dai.—Do not speak to me so bitterly—you will regret it. Had I committed some crime, you could not meet me more angrily.

Reg.—And have you not committed a crime ! Have you not laid sacrilegious hands upon the sweetest sanctities of life ? Have you not destroyed one man's faith in the goodness and loyalty of woman ? Have you not looked love with a baby innocent face, while scheming for your own advancement ?

Dai.—You wrong me cruelly—I have schemed for nothing. If I looked love, it was because I did and do love you devotedly. I would die to prove it.

Reg.—Listen, Miss Lorimer, and understand how unworthy an object I am upon which to waste your histrionic abilities. When Reginald Erly marries otherwise than as his father elected, he will no longer be the *wealthy* heir to "The Oaks." The old place will indeed be his ; but the fortune, for which you would have sold yourself, goes to Nina Dare. I—and you as my wife—would have begun married life humbly enough.

Dai.—And you intended making such a sacrifice for me ? How good you are ! It was never your fortune for which I cared, but yourself.

Reg.—Even now you count me, perhaps, a better match than the man who is waiting for you in Collinsville.

Dai.—How cruelly you insult me !

Reg.—*Do* I insult you ? Answer me truly, Daisy—when you plighted me your faith. a little while ago, were you engaged to another man ? Deny it, and I will fall at your feet and implore your pardon that I have dared to harbor so horrible a doubt against you even for a moment. You do not answer me—O Heaven !

DAI.—It is true that I was engaged.

REG.— *Was* engaged?

DAI.—*Am* engaged, horrible as it sounds. Because my grandmother wished it, I promised to marry Billy Blight, although I never professed to care for him. I never meant to deceive you—I was about to explain everything when your uncle entered the room to-day—I came here intending to tell you all my miserable story to-night; but you have heard it from others.

REG.—It was Miss Dare who told. She heard it from Dr. Mann, who has just returned from Collinsville.

DAI.—Miss Dare! Dr. Mann!—I felt certain that they were plotting against me. Miss Dare *hates* me!

REG.—It is not a question of plotting; they but repeated matter of common gossip.

DAI.—If I could but explain! If you would only listen more patiently.

REG.—What is there to explain? It is a fact that you won my love and encouraged my attentions while engaged to another man, is it not? Such a fact admits of no palliation, to my way of thinking. Mr. Blight may prove more lenient in his judgment, if you choose to confide to him this little episode in your career.

DAI.—And is this the end?

REG. —Ay, truly, the dream is broken! After to night I will see you no more, forever.

DAI. —O Rex, Rex, do not say so! [*Kneels*] Forgive me, I'm not too proud to ask it. I only know that I shall be utterly wretched without you.

REG.—Rise, Miss Lorimer, I am but a man and I love you still. If I listen to your pleadings I shall forgive you and live to be deceived again. I choose to flee from a Fool's Paradise. [*Exit* (R. 2. D.).]

DAI.—He is *gone*, but, oh, not forever! He loves me still, he said he loved me still, and he will forgive me, greatly as I have wronged him. [*Rises*] I will write to him again and again—I will beg him to return to me. [*Exit through* w.]

N𝐈.—[*Stepping to* c.] A narrow escape! Had Rex relented, all would have been lost. I did not blunder when I counted on the Erly temper. And now, Daisy Lorimer, your brief courtship is ended. Letter nor word of yours shall ever reach your lost lover, that I promise you. [*Enter* P𝐑𝐎𝐅𝐄𝐒𝐒𝐎𝐑 C. *through* w.]

D𝐑. M.—[*Aside*] Enter the Devil!

P𝐑𝐎𝐅. C. (D. c.)—I have had difficulty in joining you un-observed, my dear miss, for Judge Erly requires a great deal of my attention. He is sure to miss me before many min-utes.

N𝐈.—Our business need not take long. You have the pa-per which I requested you to return to me ?

P𝐑𝐎𝐅. C.—[*Handing paper*] Here it is, my dear miss. I have weighed its contents and comprehend its purport.

N𝐈.—And you will serve me on the terms named ?

P𝐑𝐎𝐅. C.—And why not, dear lady ? The terms are most liberal. And now let us reason together. Why should we set an undue value upon Earth-life, when Spiritual Exis-tence alone is eternal and progressive? Ah, truly, miss, we must soar upon the wings of the inspirational if we would pierce the——

N𝐈.—Oh, hush, you need play no part with me. I know that you have read the secret of my life ; but I believe I have made it clear to you that, while it will profit you nothing to betray, it will be greatly to your advantage to serve me. One question and we understand each other. You are Vol-taire Darwin's medical adviser. Do you think it probable that he will be alive, say two years from now? In other words, is he likely to live to return to America ?

P𝐑𝐎𝐅.C.—It is extremely improbable, my dear Miss. Alas ! his health is *ve–ery* frail, and so slight a thread is easily snapped. Am I obscure ?

N<small>I</small>.—No, nor am I obtuse. Enough! you must not linger here.

P<small>ROF</small>. C. —Is our good friend, Dr. Mann about? I have won in more little games with than against her.

N<small>I</small>.—Oh, she has driven over to some ridiculous woman's club!

P<small>ROF</small>. C. (<small>U. C</small>.)—[*Rubbing his hands*] That is well. let us be ecstatic and rejoice! [*Exit through* w.]

N<small>I</small>.—Poor Voltaire! Alas! the world is not large enough to hold us both. (<small>U. C</small>.) What said the honorable Professor? "His health is *ve-ery* frail, and so slight a thread is easily snapped." Ha! ha! ha! [*Exit through* w.]

D<small>R</small>. M.—[*Stepping to* c.] There was murder in that laugh, you false and bloody wretch! I will expose your infamous schemes. But what have I to go on, save my own suspi- cions? What I have *heard* amounts to nothing, and I must have proof stronger than the records of the rocks to convince that infatuated boy of Crowell's treachery. Ah, well, Vol- taire, though you will not listen to my warnings, you *shall* profit by my protecting care! (<small>U. C</small>.) And now, says I, Fred, my girl, why not follow them to Europe? Thanks to your exactions on Nina Dare, you have the means. So long as they but plotted against people for whom you did not care, you held your tongue, but now that they mean *his* ruin or death, you must follow, defy, defeat them! [*Exit* R. 2. E.]

C<small>URTAIN</small>.

ACT IV.

SCENE.—*Drawing room at " Magnolia."   Three arches sup-*
ported by columns, opening on to a covered veranda with
flowers, statuary, etc., at rear.   Upholstered circular settee
(C.).   Long mirrors (L.).   Screen (L. U. C.).   Table with
chairs, etc. (R.).   Chairs, etc. (L.).   Portrait of a gentle-
man in military dress, etc. (L.).

PROPERTIES.— *Writing materials and books on table.*

As curtain rises, DAISY LORIMER *(dressed in deep mourn-*
ing) is discovered seated at table (R.) writing.   Music plays
softly.

DAISY.--[*Putting aside writing*] It is now two years, two
long, sad years, since I have heard one kind or sympathetic
word from any one.   Oh! it is terrible to be so alone in the
world.   And I am young yet, only twenty—*so* young to be
without hope.   I seem to see my life, what is left of it,
stretch out before me, and it is very dark.   *I* shall go on
teaching year after year, growing sadder, older, thinner,
sourer, till I die at last, uncared for and unmourned.   [*Sob-*
bing] Yes, my strength is gone, and I've no heart left to
longer endure my lonely orphaned life.

[*Enter* MRS. SNIFFEN, L. D.]

MRS. SNIFFEN.--[*Aside*] Moping again! really ridicu-
lously oversensitive!   (D. C.) Are you occupied, my dear
Miss Lorimer?

DAI —I was correcting Miss Sniffen's French exercise, but
I have done.

MRS. S.—[*Seating herself opposite Daisy*] It is of Angelica Celestia I wish to speak.   I'm not quite satisfied with
her progress, my dear Miss Lorimer.   I do not wish to find

fault, but I cannot understand why the dear child has not learned *something*, during the six months in which you have been her governess. She is naturally very bright, all Vanderwhacker, no Sniffen traits—the children take after *my* family.

DAI.—But Miss Sniffen will not practise or study.

MRS. S.—How very absurd! Pray is it not your duty to contrive that the dear child *shall* practise and study? Ought you not to coax her along the difficult paths of learning, hiding the thorns from her tender feet, causing her to absorb information all unconsciously, as it were, while treading upon beds of flowery ease? Such seems to me the lofty mission of the teacher.

DAI.—It may be that I have no vocation for teaching. At all events I find it very difficult to instruct Miss Sniffen, she is so self-willed.

MRS. S.—Is not that somewhat coarsely put, or am I oversensitive? Mine is the poetic temperament that ever dreads a chill blast from the matter of fact. But I desire to be just and not to be blinded by my sensibilities. I admit that Angelica Celestia is a child of high spirit, difficult to coax and of course impossible to drive. But then her spirit is my pride, and not for worlds would I have it broken. She takes after *my* family, and the Vanderwhacker spirit was ever proud and untamed. But is it not possible there is a something lacking in yourself, my dear Miss Lorimer—tone, *dignity, je ne sais quoi?* The dear child is very susceptible to *style* and an *imposing manner*. I control her entirely by *tact, finesse, diplomacy*, possibly you are wanting in these qualities.

DAI.—Every day that I remain here I am more and more convinced that I am totally unfitted for the charge of your daughter, Mrs. Sniffen.

MRS. S.—Now don't be so absurdly oversensitive, my dear Miss Lorimer. I was not finding fault in the least, only suggesting. In many ways you have given me great satisfaction. Why, you are the first of my governesses decently young who has not driven me quite distracted, setting caps for poor dear St. Elmo.

Dai.—I have never been desirous for further intercourse with Mr. Sniffen than was absolutely unavoidable.

Mrs. S.—Darling boy, he is indeed royally endowed by nature—a child of the muses, young, handsome, and of good birth ; but that does not excuse forgetfulness of social barriers. By the way, Miss Lorimer, we are expecting a visit from the dear children's guardian and his family.

Dai.—Will their coming be likely to interfere with Miss Sniffen's studies ?

Mrs. S.—That will depend very much upon yourself, my dear Miss Lorimer. At stated times Angelica Celestia must appear in the drawing-room under your care; but I trust to you to make up to her during lesson hours for all unavoidable interruptions. And I beg of you as a favor not to refer her little playfulnesses to me, my nerves are not equal to it. I cannot tell how long Judge Erly and his family will remain with us.

Dai.—[*Starting*] Judge Erly, did you say ?

Mrs. S.—Judge Erly, of "The Oaks," the dear children's guardian, and the sole executor of my late husband's will. He has a snug little fortune, and I dare say he will make Angelica Celestia his heiress, for secretly he dotes upon the child, though one would never suspect it from his manner.

Dai.—Is Judge Erly coming *here ?*

Mrs. S.—Certainly ; you're not acquainted with the family, I suppose.

Dai.—Indeed, yes, I am ; I once visited at " The Oaks."

Mrs. S.—How extraordinary, my *dear* Miss Lorimer. Here I had always supposed you to be a mere little nobody, and it seems you have grand friends—are, perhaps, of old and distinguished family. Is it a case of fallen fortunes ? I am so absurdly romantic.

DAI.—By no means, Mrs. Sniffen ; in your sense I always was and am a *mere little nobody*.

MRS. S.—But you once visited in Judge Erly's family, you say. Was it during the lifetime of the first Mrs. Erly ?

DAI.—What do you mean, Mrs. Sniffen ? Is dear, good Mrs. Erly dead ?

MRS. S.—Why, certainly she is, these eighteen months. I never gossip, but since you know the family, there can be no harm in my telling you that the Judge has disgraced himself by marrying his late wife's waiting-maid.

DAI.—Surely *not* Ellen ?

MRS. S.—That's her name. You see she turned out to be a medium, or something of that sort, and so gained an influence over the Judge. Of course, she will accompany him here, and we must countenance her, notwithstanding she is hopelessly ignorant and vulgar. I suppose you were acquainted with Nina Dare ?

DAI.—Yes, but we were not friends.

MRS. S.—She's a mere vulgarian as to family, my dear Miss Lorimer, and *you know* what a stickler I am for blood. Had it not been for General Erly's absurd will, she must have remained in obscurity all her days, and for my part, I think he did very wrong to interfere with the designs of Providence. You see, when a mere boy, he fell in love with Nina's mother, who jilted him to marry some profligate young scamp. As might have been expected, he deserted her, and she went off in a consumption. The General adopted Nina, placed her in school, and when he died, left her to his brother's care. "The Oaks" he willed to his son, but his fortune of half a million went to him only on condition that he should marry Nina, three years his senior, on coming of age.

DAI.—Yes, I heard something of the will while I was at "The Oaks." The fortune was to go to Miss Dare if he refused to marry her, and, of course, he did, for he never pretended to care for her.

Mrs. S.—How absurdly ignorant of the world you must be to suppose such a thing for a moment, my dear Miss Lorimer! Of course, there was nothing for Rex to do but to marry his father's heiress.

Dai.—He *married* her!

Mrs. S.—Certainly; and they will be here with the others, I suppose.

Dai.—Mrs. Sniffen, I cannot remain here during this visit. [*Rises*] It is *impossible.*

Mrs. S.—You object to meeting Judge Erly's family because they knew you in days of greater prosperity? Now, that is false pride, Miss Lorimer, very wrong and very foolish, and I will not encourage it. I believe that Heaven designs to impoverish a certain number of well-bred persons, in order that the children of the Aristocracy may be served by those possessing culture and refinement, and, for my part, I think it a very beautiful expression of the thoughtful beneficence of Providence. [*Rises.*]

Dai.—Are they expected soon, Mrs. Sniffen?

Mrs. S.- Soon? Oh, to be sure! Any time—to-day perhaps. (L. U. C.) I hear a carriage on the drive this moment. [*Exit through* R. A.]

Dai.—O Heaven! Rex Erly here! and I must meet him face to face! Is there *no* escape? Nothing I can do? No-where I can go? I have often fancied what it would be like to meet him again; but never, even in my gloomiest thoughts, did I dream of finding him Nina Dare's husband. [*At table* R., *buries her face in her hands, and sobs.*]

[*Enter* REGINALD ERLY *from* R. *through* C. A.]

REGINALD (D. C.)—[*Pausing*] I beg pardon; Mrs. Sniffen directed me to this room; I did not know that it was occupied.

Dai.—[*Rising and gazing about in a bewildered way*] O Heaven! *that* voice.

Reg.—[*Starting back*] Daisy—Miss Lorimer—am I dreaming?

Dai.—Yes, it is I, Mr. Erly.

Reg.—And I never thought to meet you on this earth again. You are much changed, Miss Lorimer. I beg your pardon—that mourning dress. Is it possible that you are a widow?

Dai.—A widow! Oh, no! I am still unmarried. I have never left off wearing mourning for my grandmother.

Reg.—You are unmarried, you say. Great Heaven! I do not understand! You were engaged to be married when we parted two years ago.

Dai.—That engagement, such as it was, was broken off at once. Then came my grandmother's illness and death. I have been a governess for nearly two years.

Reg.—But I read a notice of your marriage in a Collinsville paper, two months after our parting. The belief that you were married drove me reckless. My uncle's urgent wishes, my own miserable state, property reasons, all combined to drive me into marriage with a woman I did not like, and whom I quickly learned to hate!

Dai.—I do not understand how there could have been published a notice of my marriage.

Reg.—I do, I see it all! You had left Collinsville and were off—no one knew where—alone, friendless, without means. Those who sought to injure you ran little risk. It maddens me to think how that woman has played upon my jealous passion, my violent temper, my weak credulity. But this will never do. You and I cannot play at Platonics, Daisy; we will not tamper with the Attic Bee's poisoned honey. I will leave here as soon as possible.

Dai.—Until a few minutes ago, I did not know that you were even an acquaintance of Mrs. Sniffen's. I wanted to leave here so soon as I heard that you were coming, but she would not consent.

Reg.—O Heaven! what a fool I have been! There is nothing left me now but *despair!* And you, my poor child, what will become of you?

Dai.—I shall be happier than if we had not met, Rex, for now I know that you have forgiven me.

Reg.—Ay, but çan I ever forgive myself, Daisy ? To my dying day I shall hate myself for the rage that would not let me listen to your tearful pleadings, even when I was longing to clasp you in my arms and pardon all.

Dal—Why, why did you never let me know ?

Reg.—I was about to seek you out when the news of your marriage was brought to me !

Dai.—I wrote to you, Rex, many times; but no answer ever came.

Reg.—No letter of yours ever reached me, Daisy.

Dai.—Alas! explanations are worse than useless now. We must speak to each other no more while you remain here; I cannot bear it. [*Extending her hand*] I thank you that you have restored to me my happy past, my treasure-trove, all that I have rescued from the shipwreck of my life : I must not forget that the rest is *hers*, present and future. This is good-by, Rex ; for the rest of our lives we must be as strangers.

[*Enter* Nina (r. d.).]

Reg.—[*Kissing* Daisy's *hand*] This is good-by, Daisy. For the rest of my days I shall be a wanderer on the earth —homeless and alone.

Nina (d. c.).—So you're resuming your acquaintance with my husband, Miss Lorimer? I remember that you and he were great friends at "The Oaks." I was surprised to hear that you were here as a governess. I had an impression that you were married. Ah! life is full of sad changes, Miss Lorimer, and I fear that you have had more than your share of trouble.

Dai. (u. c.)—I try to support my misfortunes with dignity, Mrs. Erly, and am no mendicant for pity.

Ni.—You're looking very much out of health, I'm sure. By the way, Mrs. Sniffen was inquiring for you.

[*Exit* DAISY *through* c. A. *to* L.]

REG.—You carry it with a high hand, madam. How dared you to step between me and the girl I loved with your lies and machinations?

NI.—How ridiculous you are, Rex. Why don't you learn to control your abominable temper?

REG.—*Now* I see it all—the intercepted letters, the false report of Miss Lorimer's marriage—*all* your shameless scheming!

NI.—So you and Miss Lorimer have been improving the time by raking up imaginary grievances. Your suspicions are absurd, of course.

REG.—I shall not remain here a moment longer than necessary, you may depend on that. You and I must live widely separated in the future.

NI.—Is there any need of creating a scandal? Mrs. Sniffen is an odious old gossip, and we may as well be careful how we indulge in recriminations here.

REG.—You need not be alarmed. I shall do nothing to create scandal. [*Exit through* c. A. *to* L.]

NI.—Impracticable fool! What cursed fate has brought us in collision with Daisy Lorimer just at this time? I cannot see what the end will be.

[*Enter* ROMEO (R. D.).]

ROMEO (D. C.)—[*Bowing profoundly*] Youse mos' obstreperous sarvant, missis.

NI.—What do you want?

ROM.—Spects you'se Mrs. Reginald Erly ob de "Oaks?"

NI.—I am.

ROM.—Perzactly so, missis. Den dar's a mos' curus gembleorum respiring for you.

[*Enter* PROFESSOR CROWELL, R. D.]

PROF. C. (D. C.).—I followed the nigger because I wanted to find you without delay, Mrs. Erly.

ROM.—[*Aside*] Nigger! Laws sakes a massy, how vulga'. [*Exit* R. D.]

Prof. C.—[*Peering about*] Are we alone, dear and honored lady?

Ni.—Entirely so—speak! Is it as I hope? For two years I have been stretched upon the rack of suspense.

Prof. C.—You remember our little agreement, dear madam, and are ready to fulfil its terms?

Ni.—Yes, yes, and now speak. Is Voltaire Darwin *dead*, and have you proof of it?

Prof. C.—I have no doubt that he has been tenderly wafted to the Summer Land, dear lady.

Ni.—But the proofs! You were not with him when he died?

Prof. C.—No; but the possibility of his living was limited to a very few hours when he managed to escape from our lodging, and I fled the country for fear of arrest and investigation.

Ni.—Where were you when you lost sight of him?

Prof. C.—In Prague. I waited at New York two weeks to hear news of his death. Words cannot express the anxiety I endured. But here is the item that set my mind at ease. [*Reads from a newspaper*] "The decease of the celebrated Medium Darwin is reported by cable. He died at the Hotel Dieu, Prague, on the third of September." [*Shaking his head*] Must have been treated for arsenical poisoning to have survived so long.

Ni.—Give me the paper, I must read it for myself. [*At table* R., *appears to read*]

[Professor C. *crosses to portrait* L., *and appears to study it.*]

Prof. C.—[*Aside*] Dress of a Confederate officer; General's epaulettes; long, gray beard; a sabre-cut over the right eye; iron-gray hair! (D. C.) Write it upon the tablets of thy memory, Confucius, my little child.

[*Enter* Romeo, R. D.]

Rom. (R. U. C.).—A permiskus individ'al ob eider sect is

promanding an ordinance wid Missis Reginald Erly, ob
de "Oaks."

[*Enter* Dr. Mann r. d.]

Dr. M.—[*Whisking* Romeo *out of the room*, r. d.] Out,
Erebus, I can announce myself!

Prof. C.—Dr. Mann, by all that is wonderful!

Dr. M.—Professor Crowell, by all that is abominable!

Ni.—[*Starting*] With what motive have you sought me
out, Frederica?

Dr. M.—That's a hospitable greeting, and after the chase
I have had to find you! When I reached "The Oaks" you
had flitted, and I followed on here post-haste. So you're
Mrs. Reginald Erly now! How's your husband, poor devil?
Ha! ha! ha!

Ni.—I shall regard this as a most unwarrantable intrusion,
if you cannot explain your business here, Frederica!

Dr. M.—Hoity-toity, not so fast! I have business, of
course, or I shouldn't have undertaken a long, expensive
journey. [*With handkerchief to her eyes*] You see I've
just heard of poor Voltaire's death, and as I'm sole executor
of the will he made before leaving America, I need a signa-
ture or two. [*Sobbing*] I suppose Crowell can give me the
particulars of his death?

, Prof. C.—[*With handkerchief to his eyes*] Alas! my good
Dr. Mann, I was not with my beloved friend at the hour of
his translation.

[*Enter* Reginald *and* Mrs. Sniffen, *followed by* Romeo
(*who remains* r. u. c.) *through* c. a.]

Mrs. S.—[*To* Reginald] What strange-looking people!
(d. c.) This naughty, *naughty* husband of yours threatens
to leave us, my dear Mrs. Erly.

Ni.—Yes, Rex is called away on important business; but
I trust he will soon be able to rejoin us.

Reg.—[*Bowing*] I have already promised our kind hostess
to return as soon as I can see my way to doing so. [*Crosses* r., *and seats himself.*]

MRS. S.—[*Aside*] They fancy they can deceive *me*—as if I didn't know there'd been a scene, and about Miss Lorimer. [*Aloud*] You have visitors, my dear Mrs. Erly.

NI.—Dr. Frederica Mann and Professor Crowell, Mrs. Sniffen. They had business with me, and have followed me from "The Oaks."

MRS. S.—I am delighted to see them; it is proverbial that our Southern hospitality is ever ready to extend the open arms of welcome, and I'm sure it's a beautiful sentiment. I should like to have you remain as my guests. [*Aside*] It's the only way in which I can find out their business here.

PROF. C.—[*Bowing profoundly*] I accept the invitation as frankly as it is given, dear and beloved lady; and may you find that in welcoming the stranger guest, you are entertaining angels unawares. I and my exalted Medicine Band have often brought down great blessings on the roof that bade us welcome.

MRS. S.—You are accompanied by friends, you say?

PROF. C.—Spirit attendants, ma'am! I trust you are not one of those who fancy that the Souls of the Departed are bottled up and hermetically sealed. Why, at this very moment, ma'am, you yourself are surrounded by an unusually large Guardian Band! One Spirit is particularly prominent. He wears the uniform of a Confederate General; his beard is long and white, his hair iron-gray, there is the scar of a sabre cut over his right eye; his arm, dear lady, is extended about you protectingly.

MRS. S.—[*With handkerchief to her eyes*] This is very affecting, Professor, for you have exactly described my late husband—General Ernest Sniffen.

PROF. C.—[*Aside*] A rich widow and fool—here's a chance. [*Aloud*] Weep not, beloved saint, but rather be ecstatic and rejoice, for it is only by soaring on the wings of the inspirational that we can ever hope to pierce the impenetrable.

MRS. S.—That's a beautiful sentiment!

[*Enter* JUDGE *and* ELLEN *through* A. *from* L.]

EL. (L. U. C.)—La! the old boy himself, and the self-made man again.

MRS. S.—I hope you will decide to remain also, Dr. Mann; we entertain the most distinguished families of our neighborhood this evening.

DR. M.—I shall admire to do so ; my baggage, with evening dress, is at the village tavern.

MRS. S. (U. C.)—It shall be sent for at once. Romeo, bring Professor Crowell's valises to the oak chamber and then go for Dr. Mann's baggage. [*Exit* (L. D.) *followed by* ROMEO *carrying valises.*]

JUDGE (D. C.)—This is a most extraordinary intrusion. I believe I made it quite clear to Dr. Mann, some two years ago, that I desired no further intercourse with her for myself nor my family.

DR. M.—Very likely you did, Judge Erly; but all that's forgotten and forgiven long ago.

JUDGE.—[*Aside*] A very objectionable female.

PROF. C.—[*Shaking* JUDGE'S *hand violently*] Have you no welcome for an humble Servant of the Spheres, Judge Erly, your old-time friend, adviser, confidant ?

JUDGE.—Humph! Rex might kick you out *now*, and I shouldn't object.

REG.—But I make it a rule never to interfere with Mrs. Reginald Erly's guests, my dear uncle.

NI. (U. C.)—Professor Crowell and Dr. Mann are no guests of mine, and if my wishes are to decide the matter, they will leave this house at once. [*Exit* (L. D.).]

DR. M.—[*Fanning herself*] Pheugh! Cool and breezy!

PROF. C.—[*Pointing to* JUDGE ERLY] But what has caused this falling from grace, my beloved hearers? Let us reason together. Has Judge Erly been faithful to that Angel Bride to whom he was united in marriage by the Spirit of the Ex-Rev. Dr. Windmere Rush? Does he continue to consult

her through the inspired Sister Tapping of Revelation
Vale?

EL.—Indeed, he doesn't! It's as much as he can do to
attend to the wishes of his lawful wife—ain't it, lovey?

JUDGE.—Humph! I've had enough of consulting *spirits*.
It's the regret of my life that I ever meddled with your
cursed little planchette.

DR. M.—Ha! ha! ha! I see it all—an excellent joke!
You made a very "natural selection"—up and married a
girl because she was a medium—and now it's a "struggle
for life" and a waiting for the "survival of the fittest."

JUDGE.—If you don't want to be made to hold your
tongue, Dr. Mann——

DR. M.—Ha! ha! ha! Let's all keep our tempers! One
of the little jokes I must have, you know.

JUDGE.—I thank Science, Professor Crowell, that I have
progressed beyond belief in the spiritual, and am no longer
to be duped by an impostor and a trickster. My investiga-
tions have led me to the Agnostic School of Evolution
and——

EL.—Now don't begin your monkey talk, Judge; nobody
wants to hear it. I'm sure I, for one, ain't related to Apes
and Baboons. leastways except by marriage. [*Seats herself
beside* REGINALD.]

JUDGE.—As Mrs. Reginald Erly has explicitly disclaimed
all responsibility in this intrusion, Professor Crowell, it is
my duty to demand your business here.

PROF. C.—It is already transacted, my good sir. At present I am in this house as Mrs. Sniffen's invited guest.

JUDGE —Humph! the deuce! But she doesn't know your
real character, sir, and——

PROF. C.—Permit me to say that you labor under a similar disadvantage yourself, Judge Erly. Your cruel suspiciousness causes me the deepest pain, and casts an imputation
upon my honor. But insult and misapprehension are ever

the portion of those who walk in the Vanguard of Truth. During the past two years I have devoted myself to the development of Spiritualism on a scientific basis. I am now engaged in photographing the human breath in the act of speaking, and my Controls assure me my experiments will soon succeed.

JUDGE.—Stuff and nonsense!

PROF. C. — What did you say, sir?

JUDGE.—[*Very loud*] I said Stuff and Nonsense!

PROF. C.—I regret to hear you say so, sir. Your scorn is owing to an imperfect comprehension of the far-reaching consequences of the idees I am seeking to develop. Without vanity, I may say that I regard my labors of the past two years as of most momentous importance to the human race. I have perfected the Telephone so that Spirits are now able to avail themselves of it for communion.

JUDGE.—Bosh and humbug!

PROF. C.—I have arranged with Edison—the greatest inventor of this or any other age, who, developing the idea . that the Universe is teeming with Voices, has taught us how they may be bottled up and uncorked at pleasure—I have arranged with him, I say, to secure the best pulpit efforts of celebrated Divines and box them up in Phonographs, when I propose making a tour of these United States, teaching the priest-ridden people how they may run their Meeting Houses by Phonograph.

DR. M.—Ha! ha! ha! You'll be tarred and feathered by a mob of the infuriated clergy, Confucius.

[*Enter* MRS. SNIFFEN (L. D.).]

PROF. C.—I have also invented a wonderful School Plan to aid in the cause of Universal Education at a Small Cost! My petition is before the Massachusetts Legislature for permission to introduce it in Boston at the public expense. I propose, my beloved hearers, to erect an immense building, to be lighted and ventilated from above. Its outer walls will be adorned with lines of elevators, fire-escapes, and entrances, while its inner ones will be honey-combed, so to speak, with tier above tier of cells to be entered from the rear. This will insure each child's being separated from his or her mates, while open to the vigilant eye of a General Inspector. These cells will be lined with zinc, and an electric attachment will enable the person in charge to send a severe shock to any refractory pupil at a moment's notice. Orders and signals can be shouted by the Areophone ; outside instructions delivered by the Telephone ; foreign languages taught with absolute perfection of accent by an immense Phonograph run by clock-work and furnished with electro-plated cylinders. Confusion will be avoided by the children reciting into the mouth-pieces of Phonographs. I see it in my mind's eye—Confucius Crowell's Bee-Hive School! the Wonder of the Century ! the Pride of Posterity ! the Triumph of Mechanism ! [*Wiping his brow*] My cerebral tissue abounds in idees enough to revolutionize this globe, my beloved hearers, and it is no wonder that the human intellect totters before the possibilities involved in these stupendous modern discoveries.

DR. M.—Ha! ha! ha! Your "Bee-Hive School" might furnish hints for a penal institute, Confucius.

MRS. S.—To me it seems a wonderful plan, founded on great originality and learning.—Would you include the Bible in your plan of instruction, Professor Crowell ? I never approved of ruling it out. You see I am a woman of great religious sentiment.

PROF. C.—The Bible, ma'am ? Certainly. And not only should the Bible be taught, but also the Talmud, the Koran, the Cabala, the Hermes. the Baghavat-Gheeta, the Precepts of Confucius, the Zend Avesta of Zoroaster, Spiritualism, and Swedenborgianism !

DR. M.—Nonsense, Confucius ; all this might be worth while, if a frog with half a brain hadn't destroyed belief in the supernatural. The coming child will be taught Baine,

Beale, Huxley, Tyndall, Spencer, Mill, Darwin, and the rest of 'em.

PROF. C.—What avails the learned ignorance of the foolish, Dr. Mann? Let us reason together. [*Sinks down on sofa,* c.]

MRS. S.—You are suffering, I fear, Professor.

PROF. C.—It is but momentary, dear and honored madam ; mere nervous exhaustion, caused by over-exertion. For the past few weeks, my beloved hearers, I have buried myself both night and day in my laboratory, putting in tangible form the last and greatest of my discoveries. By an earnest study of the life-giving principle and chemical properties inherent in food, I have discovered the essential pabulum, and invented a pill which will do away with the necessity for eating.

[*Enter* DAISY *and* ANGELICA *hand in hand.*]

JUDGE.—Cursed humbug! Would you rob us of the pleasures of the table, you rascal?

DR. M.—Reversing the spell of Circe and converting hogs into men. Ha! ha! ha! Excuse me, Judge—I must have my little jokes.

PROF. C.—[*Starting up*] My invention is meant as a boon to the poor and middle classes, Judge Erly, to whom the money and time spent in the purchase, preparation, and consumption of food are felt to be burdensome. A few of "Crowell's Patent Vitalizing Capsules," swallowed daily, will do away with any necessity for food consumption. The æsthetical development of the palate will then become a luxury of the rich.

MRS. S.—That's a beautiful sentiment. Eating would then lose its vulgarity and become a class privilege. I fear I am foolishly aristocratic in my feelings, Professor.

PROF. C.—Quite natural, dear and honored lady, it's the cry of blood!

JUDGE.—Why, here is Miss Lorimer. [*Shaking hands*

(L. U. C.)] I'm delighted to see you, my dear. (D. C.) You were a great favorite with the first Mrs. Erly.

EL.—[*Advancing and shaking hands*] La! And so she is with the second, for the matter of that.

JUDGE.—Dear, departed Saint, what a partner I lost in her! Ah! there are sad changes in this life! I regret to find you filling so onerous a position as that of a governess, my dear.

REG.—[*Aside*] It is maddening to see her in such a position.

MRS. S.—The office is a mere sinecure in our dear Miss Lorimer's case, for Angelica Celestia is her only pupil, and the dear child has a temper woven of sunbeams. Come hither, my bud of promise, and greet your guardian.

ANGELICA CELESTIA (L. U. C.).—[*Sulkily*] I shan't do it, ma; I don't care to be made a fool of.

MRS. S.—Young men are so apt to judge of what the daughters will become by what the mothers are, that I have felt it to be my duty to preserve my beauty as much as possible, my dear Judge.

JUDGE.—Poor Angelica Celestia!

[DAISY *and* ANG. CEL. *seat themselves* L.]

MRS. S.—I make Mrs. Paragon, who is a mummy at forty, furiously jealous by my youthful looks. She says scandalous things, but I enjoy it, for it gives me an opportunity to love and forgive my enemies, and that's a beautiful sentiment.

ANG. CEL.—I wish there was no such thing in the world as a sentiment.

MRS. S.—That child is *so* sprightly—all Vanderwhacker, no Sniffen traits. Both of the children inherit my poetic temperament, Judge. Angelica Celestia composed poetry at the early age of eleven.

ANG. CEL.—I beg pardon, ma; I did nothing of the sort. Compose poetry, indeed! I'm not such a fool.

MRS. S.—[*Apart*] Miss Lorimer, pray remember that Angelica Celestia is in your charge.

Dai.—[*Apart*] Pray be careful, my dear.

Mrs. S.—[*To* Dr. Mann] Miss Lorimer is sadly lacking in influence and tact.

Dr. M.—That mother-pampered little cub of yours is spoiling for a spanking.

Mrs. S.—A spanking! What a horrid, coarse sentiment!

Dr. M.—To be sure, an old-fashioned, orthodox spanking; and I'll off with my slipper and give her one for two pence!

Prof. C.—Dr. Mann is joking. Mrs. Sniffen; we hadn't ought to clip the wings of youthful genius, but let young pinions soar.

Mrs. S.—Dr. Mann knows nothing of a mother's heart!

Dr. M.—The hearts are all pretty much alike when they come to my dissecting table.

Mrs. S.—What a horrible sentiment!

El.—[*Rising*] I say, Judge, I want a walk about the grounds.

Judge.—You forget my fatigue, my dear.

El.—Oh, nonsense, come along!

Judge.—Because I am one of that sort of people who never complain——

El.—'Twouldn't make any difference if you wasn't; I'd never listen to people's aches and pains. Come on, Dr. Mann, I want you to help me look after the Judge.

Judge.—[*Aside*] Heartless woman! I've never enjoyed a day's sickness since I married her.

El.—Your arm, my dear.

Dr. M.—And lend me the other wing. Ha! ha! ha!

[*Exeunt* Judge, Ellen, *and* Dr. M. *through* c. a. *to* l.]

Mrs. S.—Let *me* introduce *you* to the beauties of " Magnolia," Professor Crowell. [u. c. *on* Professor's *arm.*] Miss Lorimer, pray bear in mind that this is the hour for Angelica Celestia's French.

A. C.—I shan't take a French lesson to-day, ma—so there now.

Dai.—Oh, yes, dear! I have a beautiful story for you to read.

Mrs. S.—[*Aside*] No tact! no influence!

Dai.—[*With excitement*] It is true! I seem to have no influence! If it is my fault——

Reg.—[*Aside*] This is unbearable!

Mrs. S.—[*To* Professor] Oversensitiveness is an odious trait in companions and governesses.

[*Exeunt* Prof. *and* Mrs. S. *through* c. a. *to* l.]

A. C.—Don't feel badly, Miss Lorimer; I'll take my lesson. Ma knows you're the only governess ever had the spunk to stay here six months, and that if she changed a hundred times, I'd never mind any one else any better. [*Winds her arm about* Daisy.]

Dai.—Then why do you behave so, my dear Angelica?

A. C. (u. c.)—Oh, because ma's such a fool.

Dai.—I'm sure it's very wrong for you to speak so of your mother.

[*Exeunt* Daisy *and* A. C. *through* c. a. *to* l.]

Reg.—How can I bear it to see her so shamefully treated? Fool, madman, that I have been; I am tied hand and foot. [*Exit* l. d.]

CURTAIN.

ACT V.

SCENE.—*Same as Act IV. Table cleared and a cover upon it. Silver pitcher and goblets conveniently placed.*

[*Enter* DR. MANN. *dragging* ROMEO.]

DR. M. (c.)—So I've caught you stealing from your mistress, eh, you black rascal?

ROMEO.—Spects you has, missis! Truf is, I has to gib my sweetheart presents same as the quality folks, and Missus Sniffen done pay mighty small wages. Certain reprobations revolve upon me as a freedman and a gembleorum and disappearances has to be kep' up. [*Snatches* DR. MANN's *handkerchief.*]

DR. MANN.—Call yourself a gentleman, eh?

ROMEO.—Parzactly so, misses. I'se a man, and a brudder under de Proclamation of Dependence and de Fifteenth Commandment.

DR. M.—Well, well, steal from Mrs. Sniffen every hour in the day, for what I care, Romeo; that was only a little joke of mine. [*Recovering her handkerchief*] I never mind people's little whims unless they interfere with *me;* but, remember, you'll get into trouble if you meddle with my belongings. I'm a constable of the peace and a private detective, do you understand?

ROM.—Laws, missis! I'll neber touch nuffin ob yourn agin, true as I draws the breff of life, almighty.

DR. M. [*Holding up a gold piece.*] – Do you know a gold piece when you see it, Romeo?

ROM.—Laws! missis, I spects des gwine fur to be common nuff now, after dis presumption ob de silber bill.

Dr. M.—What use would you make of it, if it was yours

Rom.—He! he! he! missis, I spects I'd remit alimony and set up a-housekeeping. You see I'se powerful sweet on Albina, and I 'clar fur it she precipitates. Laws! missis, when we'se togeder our two hearts beat de drum.

Dr. M.—Obey my orders and it's yours. I want you to slip down to the lodge-gate, where you will find a gentleman awaiting a message from me. Say to him that Dr. Mann wants him to accompany you back to the house. Do you understand?

Rom.—Laws! yes, missus! And I'll fotch him, sure's my name's Romeo Vanderwhacker Sniffen!

Dr. M. [*Holding out gold piece.*]—Then fly on the wings of love, you ebony angel, and earn your marriage dower! [*Exit* Romeo (l. d.).] The iron is hot, and the time has come to strike a blow! But here comes Mrs. Sniffen's "Royally Endowed"—I recognize him from his mother's description! He's worth studying. [*Steps behind screen.*] One of the little jokes I must have.

[*Enter* St. Elmo Sniffen *through* c. a. *from* r. Dr. Mann *peers out now and then during the following, and mimics* St. Elmo's *movements.*

St. Elmo.—[*Crossing* r. *and studying his appearance before mirror with absurd grimaces and bows*] Weally now, this suit is about the cowwect thing, and it can't fail to make a decided impression on Miss McStickey's heart! By Jove, my boy, you've done some execution in your day! Oh, Sainty, Sainty, you sly, solemn dog, you have a deal to answer for!—What has that yellow bwute, Ganymede, put on my mouchoir? Wiolet instead of jockey-club, by Jove! Weally I'll bweat him for it. [*Fastens the table cover to the lowest round of a chair, steps up to it and bows profoundly*] May I have the pleasure, my dear Miss McStickey? [*Waltzes around with the chair whistling. Sets it down and bows profoundly*] Thanks, my dear Miss McStickey, you have done me pwoud! [*Replaces table cover*] By Jove, Sainty, you can waltz with a girl and not step on her twain like some awkward fellahs! Miss McStickey says that my bwains are in my heels, sweet compliment to my dancing, weally! Chawming girl, Miss McStickey, charming! charming! [*Places chair on its side, and fills two goblets with water and proceeds to jump back and forth over the chair holding the goblets extended.*] Full to the bwim and you didn't spill a dwop, my boy! Now there's a steady hand, by Jove! Aw! Sainty, you can pass ice-cweam, and oysters, and such nonsense without making a muss of it like some awkward fellahs! [*Before mirror, holding a curl and sniffing*] Do I smell burnt hair? I'll thwash Ganymede if he has singed my curls again, I will, by Jove! [*Drawing on gloves*] The cwurling irons are a confounded nuisance; but then what's a poet without his ambrosial curls? [*Enter* JUDGE ERLY, R. D.] The ladies think a gweat deal of a poet, dear cweatures! Aw! Sainty, you fwascinator, there is no end of pwetty girls a-dying of love for you, and you can't make but one happy, you know, not likely!

JUDGE (L. O.)—Ahem!

ST. ELMO—[*Starting*] Aw! I was just examining to see if my twoilet was all cowwect, you know. I look all wight, how do you look? Aw! that is, my dear sir, I mean of course, *you* look all wight, how do *I* look?

JUDGE.—Like the lineal descendant of a chimpanzee, Snifty, you need not go back on Evolution.

ST. E.—Aw! weally, my dear Judge, you must excuse me, you know—some of the ladies will want to be escworted to the drawing-woom. [*Exit through* O. A. *to* R.]

JUDGE.—[*Looking after* ST. E.] There's a cerebral vacuum of very large dimensions in that poor cranium. [*Before the mirror*] What a wreck I am! It is pitiful to contemplate. Alas! time, grief, and my many infirmities are making sad ravages. These hollow cheeks, these sunken eyes, this hectic flush, [*coughs*] this hollow cough, might move the very stones to pity! [*Enter* ELLEN, L. D.] I made a precious fool of myself when I wedded a poor, friendless girl, expecting to win her love and gratitude. Ah, well! I have to thank that little demon Planchette for all my misery.

ELLEN.—[*Tapping* JUDGE *with her fan*] What are you doing, my dear; admiring your beauty, eh?

JUDGE.—[*Starting*] Ahem!—I was studying the ravages, Elaine.

EL.—Studying the ravages! ha! ha! ha! Come, that's a good joke! To be sure your beauty has gone to seed, Judge, but you can't expect to look like a young man at sixty and odd, unless you've a mind to get your wrinkles painted up and have your countenance frescoed in flesh tints.

DR. M.—[*Stepping out*] Ha! ha! ha! you've found your match at last, Judge Erly.

JUDGE.—Ma'am, you're the most audacious, pestiferous, and irrepressible female of my acquaintance.

DR. M.—Ha! ha! ha! let's all keep our tempers—you see I must have my little jokes. [*Walks about with her hands in her pockets, attracting universal attention.*]

[*Music plays back, and couples promenade behind the arches.*]

JUDGE.—If I had a wife who was willing to pay me a little of her——

EL.—Oh, nonsense, Judge, you know you said long ago you didn't want no more of my attentions!

JUDGE.—I'm not complaining, my dear. But it is a little hard, at my time of life, to be kept out of bed to see a parcel of idiots get together at an hour when decent folks are in bed, and make a night of it grimacing and capering to banjos and fiddles. I never sleep a wink after such an affair.

EL.—La! Judge, take an ethiopiate and sleep as many winks as ever you like. [*Enter* ST. ELMO *and* NINA *through* C. A.]

ST. ELMO.—By Jove, there's a gentlemanly little fellah, you know! [*Enter* REGINALD *and* MRS. SNIFFEN.]

N<small>I</small>.—That's the celebrated Dr. Mann—a strong-minded female from Boston.

E<small>L</small>.—A self-made man, Mr. Sniffen.

S<small>T</small>. E<small>L</small>.—By Jove! the very remark I was about to make, Mrs. Erly.

J<small>UDGE</small>.—Your dress is attracting great attention, Dr. Mann.

D<small>R</small>. M.—[*Whirling about*] So I flatter myself, Judge Erly. It's a very nobby affair, just made to my order by Worth, of Paris. [*All group themselves about* D<small>R</small>. M<small>ANN</small>.]

J<small>UDGE</small>.—In my opinion, a virtuous young woman should be modest in her attire.

D<small>R</small>. M.—[*Looking around at the others*] Very true, Judge Erly, very true. I always did think this stripping off of the neck and arms extremely indecorous and indelicate.

S<small>T</small>. E.—By Jove, that's just what I was about to remark!

J<small>UDGE</small>.—What the deuce, ma'am! Do you mean to insult the company?

D<small>R</small>. M.—Ha! ha! ha! Only one of my little jokes, man alive.

E<small>L</small>.—It's a Roland for an Oliver Cromwell, Judge.

M<small>RS</small>. S.—I thought ladies of the strong-minded order affected indifference to fine dress.

D<small>R</small>. M.—And why, pray? Must a woman resign claim to taste in costume because she objects to dragging a lot of senseless drapery at her heels? I'm no slave to the mandates of Fashion, but I flatter myself that, in the matter of toilet, I can do credit to any drawing-room. It's a duty one owes to society, my *dear* Mrs. Sniffen.

M<small>RS</small>. S.—That's a very right sentiment, my dear Dr. Mann.

S<small>T</small>. E.—By Jove, you know, I admire your costume immensely, Dr. Mann; but you ought to wear more jewelry.

D<small>R</small>. M.—But there isn't much jewelry to my taste, friend Sniffen. Necklaces, bracelets, and anklets are badges of the former servile condition of my sex ; bangles I resign to the ladies who love poodles, and then they'd better let the poodles wear 'em ; ear-rings are no better than nose-rings—to be sure, my auricles were pierced when I was a baby ; but I have marked my disapproval of my mother's conduct in that affair by having her portrait painted without ears. You cannot fancy how odd it looks.   Ha ! ha ! ha !

JUDGE.—Ma'am, you're outrageous.

DR. M.—Ha! ha! ha!   Joking is a bad little habit of mine, Judge Erly.

ST. E.—By Jove, I was just about to remark that, Dr. Mann.

NI.—Dr. Mann has made it the study of her life to appear eccentric, and with tolerable success.   [*Moves on with* ST. ELMO.]

[*Enter* DAISY *and* ANGELICA CELESTIA *through* C. A.]

EL.—La! Judge, here comes Miss Lorimer, and I want a little talk with her.   Just give your arm to Dr. Mann, and go promenade.

JUDGE.—With Dr. Mann, Elaine--are you crazy ?

DR. M.—[*Taking* JUDGE's *arm*] I won't poison you—come along!   It's one of the little jokes I must have. [*Exeunt* JUDGE *and* DR. MANN.   REGINALD *and* MRS. SNIF-FEN *join promenaders,* REGINALD *afterwards taking his position* L. U. C.]

EL.—Wasn't you surprised to hear I had up and married the Judge, Miss Daisy ?

DAI.—Indeed I was, and pained also, Ellen, for I heard of dear Mrs. Erly's death at the same time.

EL.--You must call me *Elaine*, my dear, the Judge won't hear to plain Ellen.   I wanted to tell you that I've tried many a time to find you, Miss Daisy ; but hearing you was married put me out.   I'll be bound that snake in the grass, Nina Dare, had something to do with the spreading of the report.

DAI.—We won't discuss it, please.

EL.—Well, then we won't. But I wanted to tell you, Miss Daisy, that the poor dear mistress—ahem! I mean of course the first Mrs. Erly—left you every bit of her china and other *bricker-backs*, and that I've packed 'em up where Nina Dare can't touch hide nor hair of 'em, to speak polite. Mrs. Erly must have been very fond of you.

DAI.—Not more so than I was of her, Elaine.

EL.—She left you her lovely little gold and green model of the Leaning Tower of Babel, Miss Daisy, and the marblette of Clytie or Psyche—I muddle the names,—but the one that married the Valentine Boy.—Judge says the story is in the Theology.

DAI.—You mean the Psyche, Elaine——

EL.—I dare say I do, my dear. I'm afraid I never open my mouth but I put my foot in it. You mustn't laugh at me, for though I've got nothing to do but polish myself up, learning ain't like burrs and don't stick. Me and Judge has has travelled all about, living on the fat of the land and dressing like queens, and I try to improve my advantages, but it's slow work. We was in New York six months putting up with the Neapolitan Hotel. I wish you could have seen it. It was ever so many floors high, but we didn't have to climb stairs, my dear. Oh, no, all we had to do was to sit in the ventilator and be histed up and down as it were.

[*Enter* PROF. *and* MRS. SNIFFEN *arm-in-arm.*]

DAISY.—Judge Erly seems to be in much better health than he used, Elaine.

[*Enter* ST. ELMO.]

EL.—He's well enough, my dear, *too* well,—I don't like to see old men over hearty. You see I broke him of his aches when once I'd married him. I just knocked his horrid little skullcap off, let in the fresh air, put anything that come to hand in his medicine glasses till I'd nearly poisoned him, and he came round amazing.

PROF. C. (D. C.)—There are very sweet and holy influences in the air to-night—I am strangely conscious of their stir-rings.

ST. E.—By Jove, you know, I was just about to remark the same thing.

MRS. S.—Have you forgotten that Angelica Celestia is in your charge, Miss Lorimer ? (U. C.)

DAI.—[*To* ELLEN] I must recall Angelica.

EL.—La ! here she comes now with Rex.

[ANG. C. *comes* D. C., *pulling* REGINALD *rudely*.]

DAI.—My dear, your mother desires you to stay by me.

[REGINALD *seats himself* R.]

ST. E.—You're looking chawming this evening, Mrs. Erly, —weally ! Won't you accept my arm for a pwomenade ?

[PROF. *and* MRS. SNIFFEN, D. C.]

EL.—La ! to be sure. I'm sick of the sight of that old corkscrew, unbottling his evil spirits. [*Raises her train by a movement of her foot*.]

[ELLEN *and* ST. ELMO *join promenaders*.]

PROF. C. (R. C.).—This is the soul's birthday of my beati-fied Aurelia, translated to the Summer-Land just seven years ago. 'Tis by her command that I wear flowers and dare rejoice.

MRS. S.—[*To* ANG. CEL.] Ah ! here you are, my bud of promise.

[DAI. *and* ANG. CEL. *seat themselves* (L.).]

PROF. C.—A very interesting child, madam.

MRS. S.—[*Seating herself* (C.)] Yes ; and strangely pre-cocious. I have always required her governesses to keep a little diary in order to record her bright and peculiar say-ings.

PROF. C.—[*Seating himself beside* MRS. S.] The *idee* does credit to your head as well as to your heart. Natural tenden-·cies are too little studied, dear and honored madam. Chil-dren should be phrenologically examined when young, by experts in craniology and physiognomics, and educated according to marked endowments, thereby avoiding wasted years of false education.

Mrs. S.—That's a beautiful sentiment, Professor; and I believe had my St. Elmo been thus studied, the world would have seen a truly great poet. He is looking radiant to-night, but I know that his heart is far from this gay scene. Ah! they are ever lonely who stand upon the heights of art, my dear Professor.

Prof. S.—[*Taking* Mrs. Sniffen's *hand*] The royal endowments of your favored children justify your pride in them, dear and honored lady. Believe me, I understand it, for should not I be the happiest of men could these gifted young beings bring themselves to see in me a proud and tender parient?

Mrs. S.—What an absurd sentiment, my dear Professor. But hush!—here comes Judge Erly.

Prof. C.—A purse-proud Aristocrat, ma'am!—a Bloated, Bond-holding Rothschild!

Mrs. S.—I greatly fear so, my dear Professor. Ah! his soul is not like mine which intuitively pays homage to the Aristocracy of Genius and Culture.

Prof. C.—[*Rising*] That's a beautiful sentiment, ma'am. I will rejoin you presently. [*Aside*] Judge Erly would not smile on this courtship of mine. [*Exit through* A. *to* L.]

Mrs. S.—I was speaking of my darling children, Judge. Do not they grow more like the Vanderwhackers every day, —no Sniffen traits?

Judge.—I agree with you, ma'am;—the Sniffens were sensible folks.

Mrs. S.—As St. Elmo's guardian, I think it would give you pleasure to read the beautiful sonnet he has composed for McStickey's album,—Miss McStickey is the great heiress, whose father made such a fortune in mucilage. The sentiment is exquisite. He compares her laughter to an Infant

Joy tumbling down a staircase of silver. Is not that fanciful and original?

DR. M.--Ha! ha! ha! It does conjure up a ludicrous image!

MRS. S.—Ludicrous? You do not comprehend the sentiment, Dr. Mann. Pray, are *you* a judge of poetry?

DR. M.—I should say so, ma'am! I once wrote reams of it; but financially it was a failure (U. C.). [*Exit through* O. A.]

MRS. S.—In my opinion, St. Elmo's verses have the sentiment of Shelley, the melancholy of Keats, the fire of Byron! My son has written for the very best magazines of the day.

A. C.—[*Between* MRS. S. *and* DAISY] And always been rejected, ma.

MRS. S.—[*Apart*] Miss Lorimer, pray remember that Angelica Celestia is in *your* charge.

DAI.—[*Apart*] Pray, be silent, my dear.

MRS. S.—St. Elmo is in correspondence with all the leading editors both North and South.

A. C.—Who always write to say that his poems are not available, ma.

MRS. S.—[*Sharply*] As I was about to explain, Angelica Celestia. It is a well-known fact that editors and publishers are the worst possible judges of what is fine in literature. Let but your brother's poems see the light--and they shall, for I mean to have them published at my own expense--and his royal endowments will be recognized. St. Elmo's appeal is to the great human heart.

[ST. ELMO *and* ELLEN *approach.*]

A. C. --What stuff you do talk, ma.

MRS. S.--Angelica Celestia, it is all very well to be sprightly, but you certainly carry it too far.

ST. E.--By Jove, I was about to make the same remark, maw!

MRS. S.—I wish you would exert some influence over Angelica Celestia, Miss Lorimer.

[DAISY *appears to expostulate with* ANG. CEL.]

ST. E.—By Jove, maw, you ought to see that natty little Dr. Mann cast sheep's eyes at me. She's stwuck! No use! I couldn't think of a female doctaw, you know—not likely!

MRS. S.—Charming, cruel boy.

ST. E.—Particularly with Mrs. Erly on my arm. 'Twould be like comparing Hy-Hy-Hyperion to a Satire.

ANG. CEL—Don't try to show off, Sainty.

ST. E.—And the pwetty little governess is fwantic with jealousy because I haven't noticed her this evening.

MRS. S.—St. Elmo is no flirt, my dear Judge; but I sometimes fear that his proud withdrawals are more dangerous to the susceptible than others' wooing arts.

ST. E.—I was about to remark something of that sort, maw—I was, by Jove!

ANG. CEL.—St. Elmo makes a perfect donkey of himself, ma, and I should think you'd have the sense to see it.

ST. E.—By Jove, you howwid, wulga', little cweature! Weally, maw, why don't you send Miss Pert to bed?

MRS. S.—[*Rising*] Don't quarrel, my darling, darling children. A sister and a brother should be like two canaries perched on one perch, cooing to each other all the day long. [*Apart*] Miss Lorimer, I desire that Angelica Celestia shall retire.

REG.—[*Aside*] This is unendurable!

[*Enter* PROFESSOR *and* NINA.]

DAI.—Let us go out on the veranda, my dear.

ANG. CEL.—I shan't stir from this room, so there now!

MRS. S.—[*Angrily*] This is your doing, Miss Lorimer. Not content with inciting my child to covert impertinence, you now encourage her to open rebellion.

REG.—[*Crossing to* L. *and standing beside* DAISY] Enough of this! I cannot and will not endure it to see you so outrageously treated, Daisy. I——

DAI.—Oh, hush! pray hush! Every word you speak only makes it worse for me.

Reg.—Too true! my interference can but injure you.
I——

Mrs. S.—If mine was not a farcically confiding nature, I
should have suspected something wrong ere this——

Ni.—Pray excuse my husband's mistaken zeal, Mrs. Sniffen. He is an old and *very intimate friend* of Miss Lorimer's, and it is quite natural he should take her part.

Mrs. S.—Miss Lorimer shall at once leave the shelter of
my outraged roof.

Judge.—[*Rising*] Silence, woman! You shall not insult
an innocent girl with impunity.

[*Enter* Voltaire Darwin, Dr. Mann, *and* Romeo *through*
c. a.; Voltaire *concealing himself behind a column.*]

Mrs. S.—This disgraceful scene in Angelica Celestia's
presence! No consideration for her tender years, her innocent heart! I shall faint!

Judge.—[*Keeping her back with his outspread hand*] Don't
you do it, ma'am, or I'll let you fall flat!

Prof. C.—[*Springing to* r. *of* Mrs. Sniffen] On this side,
dear madam—faint on this side.

Ang. Cel.—[*Clinging to* Daisy] What a fool ma does
make of herself.

St. E.—By Jove, I was just about to make a remark to
the same effect.

Dai.—[*Bewildered*] What do they all mean?

Reg.—They are a parcel of unfeeling brutes!

Dr. M. (d. c.).—Hold your tongues here, every one of
you! It is time you all know that I am in this house for a
purpose. I propose to arrest Confucius Crowell on a charge
of attempt at murder.

Ni.—[*Aside*] Great Heaven! the bolt has fallen!

Mrs. S.—Professor Crowell charged with murder! What
a horrible thought! Foolish, confiding woman that I have
been.

Prof. C.—Trust me, have faith, dear and beloved lady!

My Innocence will soon shine forth like the Unsullied Sun to overwhelm with deserved shame the Rash Accuser.

MRS. S.—Go away, you horrid, horrid man! Don't you touch me! I can't endure the sight of you.

DR. M.—I also propose to arrest Nina Dare, known as Mrs. Reginald Erly, charged with being an accomplice of Confucius Crowell's.

NI.--This is an infamous plot to ruin me!

REG.—It is my duty to protect Mrs. Reginald Erly from insult, so be careful how you bring a charge against her that you cannot sustain, Dr. Mann.

VOLTAIRE (D. C.)--This woman has no lawful claim upon you, Mr. Erly—she is my wife!

NI.—Great Heaven! Do the dead rise to accuse me?

REG.—How? What? Your wife! I do not understand.

DR. M.—Nina was this man's wife at the time of your father's death, Erly.

JUDGE.--The devil she was! Then she hasn't the shadow of a claim on the Erly name or property.

DR. M.—They were wedded when she was poor, and he a boy with prospects. The marriage was to have been kept quiet till after his consumptive father's death, but before that occurred they had quarrelled and separated.

VOL.—I make my claim now in the name of vengeance! I should never have troubled this evil woman on earth had she not put a paid assassin on my track to murder me.

REG.--Am I awaking from a long, hideous dream? [*Clasping* DAISY] Do you realize what they are saying, Daisy? I am *free*, free in all justice and honor.

NI.—I fly from here; but I leave with you, one and all, my undying curse!

DR. M.--That chicken will roost at home!—You're a prisoner and cannot leave this room. Guard the entrance, Romeo. [NINA *sinks down on chair* (R.) *with a despairing gesture.*]

EL.—La! I should think she'd have felt as if the sword of Pericles was hanging over her head all this time.

ST. E.—By Jove, I was just about to make the same remark, you know, I was, 'pon honor!

PROF. C.—Be not rash to accuse, and quick to believe evil of your old-time companion and guide, my beloved Voltaire. Consult your Spirit Friends, and they will assure you of my stainless innocence.

VOL.—You can deceive me no longer, Confucius Crowell. I had begun to suspect you of basely imitating the phenomena common at genuine séances for your own gains, when Frederica Mann discovered your deeper crime and saved my life.

PROF. C.—Frederica Mann believes that because I'm not a Bloated Aristocrat or a Bond-holding Rothschild. I'm a man who may be insulted with impunity.

DR. M.—Look here, Confucius! Do you remember the crippled hall-boy in your hotel at Prague, and your once remarking to him that he reminded of some one you had known?

PROF. C.—[*Aside*] I'm undone!

DR. M.—Oh, I can disguise myself so that my own mother wouldn't know me! This villain administered a dose of arsenic to his friend and benefactor, good folks, and then left him alone to die the death of a RAT. I found Voltaire suffering from faintness and syncope—saved his life with a dose of sulphate of zinc—carted him off to the nearest hospital, circulated a false report of his death, and then came on here to spring this trap on Confucius Crowell and Nina Dare! I can prove all I've stated, for I'm armed with marriage certificates, medical reports, affidavits, warrants, and plenty more paper amunition. [*Flings down a roll of papers.*]

PROF. C.—[*With wild gesticulation*] O Demon Diakkas, I defy and execrate your evil power, conscious that my Angel Band will quickly deliver me from your clutches.

MRS. S.—Professor Crowell may be a madman.

DR. M.—If so, he has made a great success of it financially.

EL.—I say you've did nobly, Dr. Mann, a sticking to that poor molly-coddle through thick and thin. I for one think it beautiful, to see a regular David and Goliath friendship in these nineteenth century days.

ST. E.—That's just what I was about to remark, by Jove!

JUDGE.—[*Shaking hands*] You're a deuced smart woman, ma'am, and an honor to any sex.

DR. M.—And now we must obtain a divorce for poor Voltaire, after which I shall take him in charge. I never could see that there was any immodesty or impropriety in a woman's proposing marriage to the man of her heart.

MRS. S.—What a horrid sentiment!

DR. M.—[*Taking* VOLTAIRE'S *hand*] So, my darling, if you will at last accept my love——

VOL.—I married once without the knowledge or consent of my parents, Frederica, but——

DR. M.—Never fear, love, I'll get your mother's consent this time. She's a sensible woman, and knows that you're greatly in need of some one to look after you.

ST. E.—By Jove, I was just about to make the same remark! It struck me, weally!

PROF. C.—Beloved friends, let us be ecstatic, and rejoice! Let us spread our wings and fly away! I soar after the Infinite! I dive after the Unfathomable! I wave shadowy arms towards the Illimitable! [*Waves arms wildly.*]

DR. M.—[*Grasping his hands behind and putting on handcuffs*] Come, come, Confucious, the lunacy dodge won't save you this time! Let no one interfere! I constitute myself special constable for the occasion, and arrest Confucius Crowell in the name of the Law!

ST. E.—Aw! weally! what a plucky little fellah, you know.

ANG. CEL.—[*Mimicking* ST. E.'s *manner*] As I was just about to remark, Sainty, by Jove!

PROF. C.—The power of the dark Diakkas triumphs for a time, and the influence of my Angel Band is temporarily weakened! Yet am I not dismayed. Again, and yet again have I been supernaturally rescued from the machinations of the Evil. Spirit Bride Aurelia, my Beatified, my Beautiful, I behold thee! About thy Angel head there shines a a halo of light and I read in character of fire—"The Truth is Dawning." Beloved hearers, I am ecstatic and I dare rejoice, conscious that my Innocence will soon shine forth like the Unsullied Sun to overwhelm with deserved shame the Rash Accuser.

TABLEAU.

Guests in background. NINA *at table,* R.   ROMEO, R. D.
PROFESSOR.   DR. MANN.
JUDGE.   MRS. SNIFFEN.   VOLTAIRE.   REGINALD.
ST. ELMO.   ELLEN.   DAISY.   ANG. CEL.
R.   L.

THE END.